The Angry Town of Pawnee Bluffs

The Angry Town
of
Pawnee Bluffs

LEWIS B. PATTEN

DOUBLEDAY & COMPANY, INC.

GARDEN CITY, NEW YORK

1974

Library of Congress Cataloging in Publication Data

Patten, Lewis B
  The angry town of Pawnee Bluffs.

  I. Title.
PZ4.P316An [PS3566.A79]   813'.5'4
ISBN 0-385-09602-X
Library of Congress Catalog Card Number: 74-2832

First Edition

The Angry Town of Pawnee Bluffs

CHAPTER 1

At first Sarah Lillard had been furious but now she was just plain scared. She had whipped the horses in her anger. She had made them run and now she couldn't bring them to a stop. They had the bits in their teeth and pulling back on the reins had no noticeable effect on them. Not that Sarah, who weighed only a hundred and ten pounds, could exert any great amount of pull.

The horses were probably thoroughly enjoying the run and would stop when they got tired. In the meantime, the buckboard bounced wildly back and forth from one side of the rocky road to the other, occasionally teetering perilously close to the edge where the land dropped precipitously for two hundred feet to the tumbling stream.

Sarah's fury had been directed at her father. Big, arrogant Reuben Lillard had ordered her—*ordered* her to stop seeing Jesse Marks. Otherwise, he'd said, he would see to it that Jesse lost his job. One way or another, he'd said.

Eventually the buckboard struck a rock too big to bounce over harmlessly. With a sound like a pistol shot the wheel broke. The axle dropped and dug into the ground and the buckboard overturned. The team ran on, dragging the splintered wreckage and raising a towering cloud of dust. Sarah had been thrown clear when the buckboard overturned. Now she lay, dusty, bleeding, and unconscious, ten feet from the road.

Pursuing her but two miles back her sister, eleven-year-old Melissa, did not see the wreck. But two hard-eyed, trail-dusty riders did, from a ridge half a mile away.

The men quickly glanced both ways along the road, then headed their horses down the rocky slope. They had not seen Melissa because she had been hidden by a distant bend.

Watching Sarah driving so recklessly along the road, even from a distance, they had known that she was young. And they had ascertained that she was alone.

She was still unconscious when they reached her. Her clothes were torn and her dress was pulled high above her knees. The two stared down at her for a moment, then looked at each other, something ugly taking fire in their eyes. One suddenly knelt and picked her up. At a shambling run, he carried her well away from the road and behind some rocks and brush. The other followed, grinning, leading both his companion's horse and his own. He put his back to the screen of brush and rocks and kept his eyes on the road.

After a while the first man emerged. The second man's grin faded and he disappeared behind the rocks. Sarah Lillard came to and began to scream.

Melissa, approaching along the road at a gallop, heard her sister's screams before she reached the place where the buckboard had overturned. White-faced and scared, she rode toward the dirty, hard-faced man keeping watch. She had never seen him before.

Before she could speak, he yanked her brutally off her horse. She hit the ground on her back. It knocked the breath out of her but as soon as she could she, too, began to scream. He yanked her up and hit her with his fist.

Behind the screen of brush and rocks, Sarah suddenly now was still. The second man emerged, his dirty face shining with sweat. He grunted, then said, "What are we goin' to do with 'em? When they tell what we done . . ."

"They ain't going to tell. They're going off the edge. Who's to know they didn't go over when the buckboard wrecked?"

The other man said, "That one ain't very old."

"She's old enough to talk. Get up on your horse where you can see and keep an eye on the road. When I've gotten rid of this one I'll come back for the other." He carried Melissa down to the road and across. As if she were an armload of trash, he pitched her over the edge.

He hurried back. First he gathered up Sarah's clothes. Then he picked her up—easily. He carried her to the edge and threw her over. He tossed her torn clothes after her.

Turning, he yanked a branch from a clump of sagebrush and brushed out his boot tracks in the road. Throwing it aside, he returned to the rocks and mounted his horse. The two rode straight away from the road and disappeared over the rocky ridge.

Half a mile along the road leading to the town of Pawnee Bluffs, the team was now quietly cropping grass. In the canyon, the tumbling stream gave off a muted, steady roar. Everything else was still.

Sarah's first awareness was of cold. The second was of pain. She was lying half in, half out of the icy creek. She groaned and tried to pull herself out of the water, with only indifferent success.

She could see her body when she raised her head and the sight of it horrified her. It was a mass of ugly bruises and of cuts and abrasions from which blood had run and, where it had been out of the water, dried. For several long moments all she could remember was the wreck. She had been thrown over the cliff, she thought. She had fallen to the bottom, striking the canyon wall repeatedly, and perhaps that was the reason she had survived. The bumps against the canyon wall on the way down had slowed her descent enough so that she had not been killed when she finally reached the bottom.

But there was something . . . something like a nightmare in the back of her consciousness. Something even worse than the fall had happened to her only she could not remember what it had been.

It was late afternoon. The sun had set here in the canyon and that accounted for the cold, but she could see it still shining out on the prairie several miles away.

With great effort and the help of a nearby rock, she pulled herself to her feet. Steadying herself, she glanced toward the road, two hundred feet above. She would have to climb back up because she couldn't go down the stream. Not without getting drowned.

A spot of color caught her eye. It was what was left of her skirt. She staggered to it and picked it up. It had not fallen in the water and was therefore dry. She arranged it so that it partially covered her. A dozen feet above her, caught on a bush, was the torn remains of her blouse. She struggled up toward it, and when she reached it she put it on, tying the torn ends so that it covered her.

In constant pain, often crying out, she struggled on, knowing that she had to reach the top before it got dark. Out on the plain, the sunlight disappeared. Here in the canyon, it grew darker as dusk settled upon the land.

Sarah didn't know how long it took her to reach the top. Three times she almost fell when rocks slid out from beneath her feet. In complete darkness she crawled out on level ground and lay there, panting and exhausted, too tired and in too much pain to care.

She must have either lost consciousness or slept. When she raised her head she saw the light of lanterns and heard men's voices. A sudden, terrible fear came over her. She wanted to hide from them but there was nowhere she could hide. As the lanterns and voices approached, Sarah tried to cower closer to the earth. She didn't know why she was afraid, but she was.

When they found her, and touched her, she began to scream. She screamed and fought until finally, cradled and held in big Reuben Lillard's arms, she lost consciousness again, too exhausted to scream any more.

Jesse Marks was alone in the sheriff's office when Lillard's man arrived. He had his feet up on the desk. When Lillard's rider, a man named Jed Brown, came bursting in, he put his feet on the floor and straightened up.

Marks was a big young man, six feet two inches tall. He weighed an even two hundred pounds and looked neither as big nor as strong as he really was. He was yellow-haired and had soft brown eyes that could, on occasion, turn surprisingly hard.

Brown said excitedly, "Sarah's hurt! Her buckboard wrecked and she was throwed off the cliff."

"Where is she now?" Jesse's eyes showed his shock.

"The boss is bringing her in. He sent me ahead to have Doc Peabody get ready for her."

"How bad is she hurt?"

"I don't know. She's banged up from the fall. Her clothes was purt near tore off o' her. She was screechin' when I left."

"Screeching?"

"Yeah. Damndest thing. When they touched her she commenced to screech like they was killing her."

"Where was she when they found her?"

"Layin' near the road. She must've climbed back up after she was throwed off the cliff."

Marks let out his breath with relief. "Then she can't be hurt too bad."

"You wouldn't say that if you could've seen her."

Marks nodded. "All right. Thanks." Brown went hurrying out the door. Marks stood at the window, staring after him. Behind him, the office clock ticked. He looked at it; it was almost ten o'clock.

He felt as if he had been slugged. He was numb at the thought of Sarah being hurt. He wanted to get a horse and ride out to meet them but he resisted the idea. Sarah's father would be understandably upset. He'd start a quarrel and Marks didn't want to fight with him while Sarah was lying hurt. But he ached to see her and comfort her.

He blew out the lamp and closed and locked the door. He hurried up the street toward Doc Peabody's house, at its upper end. There were lamps burning all through the house. The front door was open and Doc was waiting on the porch. He said, "Brown came and told you, huh?"

"Uh-huh." Marks was silent for a moment, then said hopefully, "Brown said she climbed up out of the gorge. She couldn't do that if she was real bad hurt, could she?"

"Likely not," Peabody said comfortingly.

Marks asked, "How the hell could anybody live through a fall like that?"

"Maybe it wasn't very deep where she went off."

"There's only one place where the road's close enough for her to get thrown over, and right there it's two hundred feet straight down."

"Then the Lord must've been looking after her."

Marks left him and walked out to the street. He peered in the direction from which he knew they'd come. He heard hoofbeats, finally, and the grating of a buckboard's wheels.

Several riders came into view, then the buckboard, with one man driving, and Reuben Lillard sitting next to him on the seat, his daughter cradled in his arms. Marks stepped close as the buckboard halted, holding up his arms to take her, but Reuben said with harsh fury, "Get out of my way, you son-of-a-bitch. If it wasn't for you, this wouldn't have happened to her!"

Anger touched Jesse Marks. But he stepped aside and Reuben handed his daughter down to one of his men, who quickly turned and carried her inside. She showed no sign of consciousness. Her clothes hung from her body in rags.

Reuben stalked after the man carrying her. The door of Doc's house closed.

In the darkness Marks looked at the members of Reuben's crew, clustered near the tailgate of the buckboard, holding their horses' reins. He asked, "What happened?"

Galen Sauls was Lillard's foreman and he liked Marks though he never showed it when the old man was around. He said, "They had a row this afternoon."

"About me?"

"Uh-huh. The old man told her if she saw you again he'd see that you lost your job."

Marks didn't say anything. The fight Reuben and Sarah had had explained Reuben's accusation a few minutes ago.

Sauls said, "She left, driving the buckboard. She was pretty mad. I figure she must've got the horses running after she got out of sight of the ranch. Maybe she couldn't make 'em stop. That team likes to run and if they get the bits in their teeth it takes someone stronger than Sarah to make 'em stop."

Marks suddenly realized that he hadn't seen Melissa. He asked, "Where's Melissa?"

There was a moment of dead silence. Then Sauls said, "Oh God, I wonder . . ."

"What do you mean? Where is she?"

"She left on horseback right after Sarah did."

"Did her horse come back?"

"I don't know. He wasn't back before we left."

"Didn't anybody miss her?"

"Maybe the old man thought about it, but I reckon the way Sarah was carryin' on put it plumb out of his mind."

"What did you do with the buckboard team?"

"I turned 'em loose. I figured if I didn't the old man might shoot 'em both before he got cooled off."

"Could Melissa's horse have been somewhere nearby?"

"Could have."

"Without you seeing him?"

"Could be. But he'd have headed on home with the buckboard team after I turned 'em loose."

Marks said, "I think we'd better get a search party up and go look for her. One of you go wake the sheriff up. Some more of you get Rittenhouse to open the store and get some more lanterns and ropes. The rest of you roust out enough men to do some good."

They dispersed rapidly. Jesse Marks headed for the livery stable to get his horse. He was anxious about Sarah and wanted to be with her but he knew that Reuben Lillard wouldn't permit it. He also knew that she was getting the best care available.

The best he could do for her right now was to try to find out what had happened to Melissa, if anything.

CHAPTER 2

The sheriff, Morgan Keogh, was a powerful man, five feet six with broad shoulders and a chest like that of a bull. His legs looked both too short and too slight to support the rest of him, but they'd been supporting him for sixty years and weren't likely to stop doing so at this late date. He weighed two hundred and ten pounds but he looked heavier.

He rode his big, hammerheaded gray to the jail. He stepped down ponderously and spoke to Jesse Marks. "Do you know for sure that Melissa Lillard is missing?"

"No. I just think she is. Sauls said she followed her sister this afternoon and didn't come back."

"What were they having, some kind of row?"

Jesse nodded. "About Sarah seeing me."

"And you think Melissa might have caught up and gone off the edge when her sister did?"

"It could be what happened," Jesse said. Now that he thought about it, though, it seemed less likely, particularly since the buckboard hadn't gone off the edge.

"And you haven't talked either to Sarah or her pa?"

"Her old man won't talk to me, except to cuss me out. And it looked like Sarah was either unconscious or asleep."

"All right. Stay here and get the men together. I'll be back."

When he returned there were a dozen men with horses in front of the jail. "She's missing all right. You take about half these men and ride downstream from the bridge. I'll take the rest up where the buckboard was wrecked and work back from there."

Jesse untied and mounted his horse. The sheriff called off half a dozen names and those he had called followed him down the street. The others, some with ropes or lanterns or both, followed Jesse toward the bridge at the lower end of town.

The town of Pawnee Bluffs was built on rolling prairie a mile from where the road came twisting down out of the mountains. It took its name from two steep, broad-faced mounds, one on each side of the road, which had been a land-mark for the early settlers moving west. They stood about halfway between the town and the first upthrusting hills. Their origin was unknown but people often speculated about how they might have been formed. From a distance they re-sembled a sleeping woman's breasts and the town might have had another, less respectable name if its founders had been willing to take themselves less seriously, because the first white men to see the Pawnee Bluffs had not called them that. They had been given that name later because of their resemblance to the dwellings of Pawnee Indians.

At the bridge, Jesse Marks split his force, sending three down one side of the creek, three more down the other. He himself took a lantern from one of the men and forced his horse out into the stream.

It was not the brawling, tumbling stream here that it was in the mountain gorge. It flowed quietly over a bottom where there were few rocks bigger than a man's head, and its width was double what it was where Sarah Lillard had fallen into it. Lining its banks were scrub cottonwoods and clumps of willow, and frequently there were pileups of dead sticks and brush. It was possible that Melissa, if she had been swept downstream, had been caught on one of these.

It was Jesse who found her, and she had, indeed, caught

on some snags. He rode his horse to her and dismounted. The water came halfway up his thighs. He hung the lantern on a dead branch immediately above her, then gently dislodged her body from the snags on which her clothes were caught. She was cold and stiff and seemed incredibly small—much smaller than she had in life. He freed her and laid her across his saddle. He called out, "I've found her!" and mounted behind her, then took the lantern from where he had hung it earlier. He rode out of the stream, handed the lantern to the first man he met, then raised Melissa's body and cradled it in his arms.

Jesse Marks was in love with Sarah Lillard, but he had loved Melissa, too. She had been sweet, and very young, and one of the few people who had thought Sarah ought to marry him.

One of the men riding with him said, "I'll ride up and tell the sheriff." He galloped away. Reaching town, Marks rode straight toward Doc Peabody's, but he never got that far. Galen Sauls met him, took Melissa's body from him, and headed back toward Peabody's.

Ernst Halverson, one of those who had ridden with Jesse, said, "Come on. I'll open the saloon. I think all of us could use a drink."

Jesse's legs were wet and cold. His mind felt numb. He dismounted in front of Halverson's Pawnee Saloon, tied his horse, and followed the others in. Water sloshed inside his boots, squishing with every step. He sat down in a chair and got one of the men to help him pull them off, then poured the water out on the floor and put them back on his feet.

He went to the bar and Halverson slid him a bottle and glass. Jesse drank the first one in a couple of gulps and poured a second. He was horrified. How could both girls have been thrown off the cliff and the buckboard have stayed up on the road?

Jesse Marks was thirty-one. He hadn't been a law officer nearly as long as Sheriff Morgan Keogh had, but he'd been one long enough to get a certain feeling when something wasn't right. He had that feeling now. Melissa had ridden after Sarah, but it shouldn't have been *after* she caught up that Sarah's anger made her whip the team into a run. It should have been before. And if Sarah had managed to stop the team of runaways once, she wouldn't have permitted them to run a second time. Nor would they, probably, have wanted to.

Tomorrow, at first light, he'd ride up where the buckboard had been wrecked and look around. The tracks would be all messed up, first by Reuben Lillard and his men, who had found Sarah, and second by the sheriff and the half-dozen men he'd taken to look for Melissa. But there might be enough tracks left so a man could tell what had really happened there.

He finished his drink, then went out and led his horse down the street to the jail. After a while Keogh came in. He said, "Good work, finding her so soon." He studied Jesse's face. "You'd better get some sleep. You look like hell."

Jesse Marks went out. He didn't say anything about what he meant to do at dawn because he knew he might be wrong. He rode his horse to the livery stable and put him in a stall.

He had a room at Mrs. Willet's Boarding House. The place was dark. Feeling his way, he went up the stairs. He didn't bother to light the lamp. He draped his pants over the chair so they'd dry during the night. Then, in his underwear, he crawled into bed.

It was a long time before he slept. He blamed Reuben Lillard for what had happened to Sarah and Melissa. If the old bastard wasn't so damned bullheaded and mean . . .

He didn't know what he was going to do. He wasn't going to give up Sarah as long as she wanted him. Maybe, when she was better, they ought to just run away to some nearby town and get married. He wondered what Reuben Lillard would do if they did.

He finally went to sleep, promising himself that he'd see Sarah when he got back to town tomorrow no matter what Reuben Lillard said.

Jesse Marks was up half an hour before first light. He felt his way downstairs and went out into the chilly, fresh-smelling morning air. He wondered how Sarah was.

He got his horse at the deserted livery stable and saddled him. He rode out of town at a steady trot.

He reached the shelf road as the sky was beginning to turn gray, and halted by the wreckage of the buckboard. Here, he waited until it was light enough to see the ground.

Slowly studying the road as he did so, he retraced the team's path by the deep scratches left in the road by the shattered buckboard. Less than a mile farther on, he found the pieces of the broken wheel where the wreck had occurred.

He dismounted. There were hundreds of tracks in the road and between the road and the cliff. There was no way of ascertaining anything, not even where Sarah had been found. Frowning, he noted where the axle had first dug into the road and, a little farther on, the deep gouges where the buckboard had overturned. He should have felt satisfaction at discovering it, but he only felt a deepening alarm. The wheel that had shattered had been on the side away from the cliff and the buckboard had flipped away from the cliff rather than toward it. There was no way anyone in the buckboard could have been pitched off the cliff as a result of the wreck.

The sun was now staining a few high clouds in the east. Jesse Marks headed away from the road, studying the ground as he walked. For twenty-five or thirty feet there was an abundance of tracks, all having been made either by Reuben

Lillard's men or by the sheriff and his search party last night. Marks kept going and finally was rewarded by finding a double set of tracks made by horses who had approached the wreck and then gone away from it. He also found boot tracks made by boots with holes in the soles and run-down heels.

By now, Jesse's feeling of dread was increasing by leaps and bounds. He reached a screen of brush and rocks and found where horses had stood and fidgeted for a time and where a man, also, had waited, fidgeting.

He went behind the rocks and brush and instantly knew that his dread had been justified. Here were the marks of a struggle, and several scraps of cloth that could only have come from Sarah's dress and petticoat. He picked up one scrap that looked as if it had come from her dress. He left the other scraps where they were.

Eyes narrowed and hard as nails, Jesse circled until he found the tracks of the two horses going away. They headed straight up the rocky ridge, deeply indented as if the horses had been lunging up the slope instead of simply climbing it.

Jesse stopped. The blood was pounding in his head. He knew, now, what had happened here yesterday. The buckboard had been wrecked. Two men, watching, had seized Sarah and brought her behind the screen of brush and rocks. Both had raped her and then one of them had thrown her off the cliff. Melissa must have caught them doing it, and they'd thrown her over, too.

Trembling, fists clenched, he stood there as if rooted to the ground. Every nerve, every muscle, screamed for him to ride, to catch the men, to exact a vengeance as terrible as what they had done to the girls.

Only his years as a lawman kept him still while his tortured mind considered the alternatives. He knew it had happened yesterday afternoon. If he had been the two men, having done what they had done, he would have ridden all through the night. Which meant that they might well have a start of as much as fifty miles.

No. He must return to town, tell the sheriff what had happened, and let him raise a posse and go after the men. Keogh wouldn't think of denying him the chance to go along. Keogh knew how he felt about Sarah.

Even with his decision made, he had to force himself to walk back to where he had left his horse. He felt alternately hot and cold. His head ached with the intensity of his hatred and revulsion. They'd thrown the two girls, like used-up trash, to what they had thought would be their deaths. Only by a miracle had Sarah survived the fall.

He swung to the saddle and sank his spurs hard into the sides of the startled horse. Recklessly he thundered down the road.

CHAPTER 3

No news had ever before spread so swiftly through the town of Pawnee Bluffs. Like a fire in dry prairie grass, it swept across the town, bringing the people from their houses and down into the center part of town. Men came armed and with horses, blankets, and provisions, ready to ride with the posse they knew would be organized. Women came to Doc Peabody's house with broth and soup for Sarah, until there was enough broth and soup in Mrs. Peabody's kitchen to feed the whole family for a month. Others who could came driving buggies and headed out the road to the LL ranch to comfort Mrs. Lillard. That they met her driving a mile from town diminished in no way their kindly intentions, and they followed along behind, prepared to give whatever sympathy and comfort that they could.

In the sheriff's office, which adjoined the jail, Morgan Keogh furiously paced back and forth, impatient with the delay. Once, he looked at Marks. "You got a fresh horse all ready to go?"

"Yes, sir. And I got one for you."

"What about grub? Did you take care of that?"

"I got enough to last a five-man posse for a couple of weeks. I got a packhorse and loaded him with food and ammunition and blankets. If we take more than five men, they can bring some of their own."

"All right." Marks had never seen Keogh so angry. He had

never been so angry himself. He had never even heard of such a brutal, callous crime.

A couple of riders halted out front, dismounted, and tied. Keogh looked at Marks again. "You're sure? There can't be no mistake?"

Marks said, "No mistake. I found the place they . . . well, I found the place. There's no way those girls could've got over that cliff unless they were thrown over."

"Maybe they were running. Maybe they jumped off, or fell off while they were trying to get away."

"No, sir. Nobody jumps off a cliff—not one that's two hundred feet high."

"No. I guess not. It's just hard to believe there's men like that."

Marks said, "We'll be going out there to pick up the trail. You can look over the ground. You can make sure I didn't make a mistake."

Keogh nodded. Marks knew he would go carefully over the ground despite his anger and sense of urgency. Keogh didn't go off half-cocked, and he would not let his fury make him do so now.

More men pulled up in front. Several were members of Lillard's crew. One was his foreman, Galen Sauls. Marks stepped outside and asked, "Is Mr. Lillard going along?"

Sauls shook his head. "He wanted to, but I talked him out of it. I told him Mrs. Lillard and Sarah needed him."

Jesse asked, "What about me? Do you think Sarah would see me before we go?"

Sauls said, "She might, but the old man wouldn't let you in without a fight. Better let it go until we get back."

"Is she going to be all right?"

Sauls said, "Doc says she is. He don't know why, but she hasn't got any broken bones. He says all she needs is time, and rest."

Jesse Marks didn't say anything about Sarah's state of mind. More had happened to her than a fall two hundred feet down the cliff. What had happened to her before the fall had been much worse than the fall itself.

Thinking about that made his face feel hot with anger and his hands begin to shake. Several more men showed up in front. Now there were an even dozen. With Keogh and Marks, that made fourteen. An unwieldy posse, but Marks doubted if any of the twelve men outside was going to be denied. Apparently Keogh thought that too because he didn't try to persuade any of them not to go. He only said, "We're going to be riding hard. Anybody that can't make it will be left behind. Is that clear?"

All the men agreed. Keogh said, "Raise your right hands."

The men did, impatiently. Keogh said, "Do you solemnly swear to uphold the laws of this state and county to the best of your ability?"

"We do." The reply came raggedly.

Keogh said, "And that means doing what I say. There is not going to be a lynching. Is that clear?"

There was a grumbled murmur that might have been taken as either agreement or disagreement. Keogh chose not to make an issue of it. He untied his horse and swung ponderously to the animal's back, hitting the saddle with a thud. Jesse Marks untied his animal and mounted. He wheeled the horse and led the posse out of town at a canter, trailing the packhorse behind. The others came along, raising a cloud of dust that lay over the street like a pall. Citizens stood on the walks, staring at the posse with grim approval. There were no shouts or cheering, and no exhortations to the posse members. The town was silently furious, individually and collectively.

Marks glanced at Keogh's face. It was set and hard, and angry, too. Jesse Marks turned his head and looked behind at the other men. The same expression was on all their faces. Angry men. Determined men. Dangerous men.

Despite his own anger, his own outrage, his own determination that the rapists and killers be caught and brought to justice, Jesse Marks felt a stirring of uneasiness. In their present mood these possemen might well insist on lynching, immediately upon catching up with them, the men who had killed Melissa and raped Sarah. Keogh would, of course, refuse to permit it. Jesse would have to side with him. And that might result in a confrontation—twelve angry men against two equally angry lawmen whose oaths refused to permit such a violation of the law.

If they lost, only the bodies of the two criminals would ever reach Pawnee Bluffs. If they won, the prisoners would come in, trussed and helpless, to face the combined fury of every citizen of the town and the surrounding countryside. And there would be another confrontation between those who would hang the prisoners and the sheriff and his deputy, who could not permit them to.

He shrugged irritably. The two men were at least fifty miles ahead. They weren't going to close that distance and catch the men for a couple of days. By that time the possemen would be tired. Their anger would have cooled. They might be a lot more reasonable.

They reached the site of the attack after less than an hour's ride. Keogh directed the possemen to stay on the road beside the wrecked buckboard while he and Jesse slowly rode forward to read the tracks.

Jesse pointed out that all the tracks that might have been in the road and between the road and the cliff had been obliterated by Reuben Lillard's crew, searching for the girls, and later by Keogh's own men, searching for Melissa. He led Keogh to the spot behind the screen of brush and rocks where

Sarah had been raped before being thrown off the cliff. Some scraps of her torn clothing still lay scattered around.

Jesse looked at Keogh's face. He had never seen it so furious. Keogh's eyes blazed. His mouth was a thin, straight line. Much of Jesse's own fury had spent itself earlier and, like a fire, had died to slow-burning coals. Jesse was in love with Sarah. The thought of her stripped and manhandled by two dirty brutes here on the ground was almost more than he could stand. It was like a knife turning in his gut. He looked at the sheriff and asked, "Seen enough?"

Keogh's angry eyes studied him for a moment. He said, "I'm going to bring them back. I want them to go to trial. I want them to hang but I want it done legally. I don't want you shooting them. Is that understood? Otherwise you can go back now."

Jesse said, "I'm not going to shoot them. That's too easy a way out for them."

"All right, then, let's get at it."

He beckoned to the other members of the posse. He brought them to where the attack on Sarah had taken place and he carefully pointed out the marks on the ground, the torn scraps of clothing, so that their testimony could be used later as evidence at the trial. Jesse couldn't stand to listen. He rode away, taking the trail the two had made when leaving the spot. It led up through the rocks, in places hard to follow. At the top of the ridge the trail lined out straight away from where Sarah had been attacked, heading west toward the high peaks lifting their heads in the distance.

Jesse held his horse to a steady trot, a mile-eating gait that was very easy on horses and could be maintained for hours without tiring them. His thoughts were seething and his head ached ferociously. He was thinking of all the things he wanted to do to the pair. He wanted to mutilate them so that they would never attack another woman. He wanted to kill them but he wanted to do it in such a way that before they died they would suffer the way Sarah had suffered.

It still was incredible that Sarah had survived both the attacks and the fall to the bottom of the cliff. Her body would mend in time, he knew. But what of her mind? Could she forget what had happened? Could she ever stop blaming herself for Melissa's death, because if she had not driven away from home angry, Melissa would not have followed and would now be alive. These would be the things Sarah would be telling herself. She might even blame him because it was a fight over him that had precipitated everything.

Coming on at a lope, the other members of the posse caught up with him. Keogh took his place beside Jesse. The fourteen-man posse swept on, raising a towering cloud of dust. Jesse turned the packhorse over to one of the others so that he could concentrate on the trail.

Jesse was an expert tracker and so was Morgan Keogh. Unless it rained, which was unlikely, they weren't going to lose the trail. It was only a matter of time until they caught up with the fugitives.

Reuben Lillard glanced up as his wife came into the parlor of Doc Peabody's house. His eyes were cold. He did not rise and go to her, and indeed she did not expect him to.

They had been married for twenty-two years. In spite of the fact that they had produced two children, it had not been a marriage of love. Reuben Lillard had loved another woman before he'd met Mary Lillard, a woman Morgan Keogh had married. Two years later she had been accidentally killed by a bullet meant for Morgan.

Reuben Lillard had never forgiven Morgan Keogh for her death. For twenty-five years they had lived here in the same community. They gave every outward appearance of getting along. Yet both knew it was a sham. Lillard hated Keogh.

Keogh knew he did. Lillard's refusal to let Sarah marry Jesse Marks was a manifestation of that hate. He justified it by telling her that he didn't want her dying from a bullet meant for Marks. But that was, at least in part, another sham.

Mary Lillard sat down quietly in a straight-backed chair. She looked at her husband. She seemed timid but there was a surprising reservoir of strength in her. She asked softly, "How is Sarah?"

"It's a miracle that she's still alive."

"Have you spoken to her?"

He shook his head.

The door opened and Doc Peabody came into the room. He looked at Mary Lillard and said, "Good morning, Mrs. Lillard."

"Good morning, Doctor. How is Sarah?"

He gave her a professional reply. "She has no broken bones. She has a good many bruises and abrasions, and a mild concussion, but there is nothing from which she cannot recover."

Mary Lillard studied his face, reading in it all the things the doctor would not say. More had happened to Sarah than the fall. Her body might recover but the scars on her mind might never heal. Mary said, "I suppose Jesse Marks has gone after them."

Doc Peabody nodded. Reuben Lillard scowled, started to say something, then changed his mind. Mary Lillard said, "I wish that he had stayed. I think she needs him now."

Peabody did not reply. He was watching Reuben Lillard warily. He couldn't decide whether or not Mary Lillard was baiting her husband by mentioning Jesse Marks. He did know that mention of Jesse's name made Lillard even more furious. He glanced perplexedly from one to the other and then left the room. He returned five minutes later and spoke to Mary Lillard. "She would like to see you, Mrs. Lillard."

Mary rose. Reuben asked, "What about me?"

Peabody shook his head. Reuben said, "I'm going in. It's my right. . . ."

Peabody was three inches shorter than Reuben was. He was slight, except for a modest paunch. He stood between Reuben and the open door behind him and said, "No. Stay here, Mr. Lillard. She wants her mother now." The words were reasonable but there was steel in Peabody's voice. Lillard turned away, grumbling to himself. He began to angrily pace back and forth. Peabody went into another room that opened off the parlor, which he used as his office.

From the adjoining room, where Sarah was in bed, Peabody heard the sound of their voices and, a little later, the awful, tearing sounds of Sarah's sobs.

He sat down in his office, filled with pity for the girl but pleased that her cold, almost numb restraint had finally given way. It would do her good to weep.

CHAPTER 4

They found the killers' first-night's camp less than twenty miles from where the attack on Sarah and Melissa had taken place. The fugitives seemed to be traveling at an almost leisurely pace, sure, Jesse supposed, that both girls were dead and that it would be assumed they had been accidentally thrown over the cliff when the buckboard overturned. They hadn't bothered to notice which way the buckboard had flipped. Had it gone the other way, it was indeed possible that everybody would have assumed the girls had been thrown over in the crash. Later, Sarah would have remembered what had happened, and would have told, but by then it would have been too late to ever find the men.

The posse was now less than four hours behind. If the pair continued to travel as leisurely as they had so far, they would catch up with them no later than early dark.

Jesse Marks felt the sheriff watching him, but every time he turned his head the sheriff looked away. Finally he said irritably, "Something on your mind?"

Keogh said, "Sorry," without pretending that he hadn't been watching his deputy.

Marks liked and admired Morgan Keogh. He knew that a gigantic battle of wills was going to take place when they got back to Pawnee Bluffs with the prisoners. Reuben Lillard would fight, with every means at his disposal, to keep the matter from ever coming to trial because if it did Sarah would be called as a witness, something bound to be devastating for her. Keogh would fight with all *his* strength to keep the prisoners safe and bring them to trial properly. That was his job. And, despite any conflicting feelings he might have, it was also the job of Jesse Marks.

He turned his head and looked at the posse members, sweeping along behind, their horses held to a steady trot. They were strung out now for several hundred yards but he could see enough of their faces to know that their anger and sense of outrage remained. Each knew their own wives or daughters could have been the victims instead of Sarah and Melissa. With men as cold-blooded as the two they were pursuing, the attack on Sarah and Melissa could not have been the first and wouldn't be the last. Other women and girls had died at their hands, and still others would die unless they were caught.

The possemen were coldly angry now, but how would they be when the men finally were caught? Jesse glanced at Keogh again, noting for the first time that the stock of the sheriff's double-barreled shotgun, instead of his rifle, protruded from the saddle boot. Keogh's thinking was obviously the same as his, since a shotgun was useless against fugitives. The shotgun was there in case the posse members decided to take matters into their own hands. Keogh had been watching him because he was wondering which side Jesse would be on.

Jesse examined his own inner feelings, trying to decide that question for himself. It was easy, now, to say he would side with Keogh and insist on bringing the prisoners back to Pawnee Bluffs for trial. But what would happen to him when he actually stood before the two men, looked into their faces and their eyes and remembered what they had done to Sarah before they so callously threw her off the cliff? How would he feel then and what would he do? Just thinking about it made his heart beat faster, made his face feel hot and his hands begin to shake.

He opened his mouth to tell Keogh he needn't worry, then closed it again without saying anything. He didn't have to reassure the sheriff that his intentions were good. Keogh knew that much. What Keogh wanted to know and had to know was something Jesse Marks couldn't tell him yet.

He found himself thinking of Sarah, imagining her terror and helplessness. He wondered how many of her bruises had been caused by her attackers' fists and how many by the fall. He had to force himself to stop thinking about it because he kept getting progressively angrier and more irrational.

Noon came, and Keogh halted the men. He ordered everyone to unsaddle and cool their horses' backs. He let them eat, but only cold food because he not only didn't want to take time for fires but he didn't want to risk the chance that the fugitives might see the smoke.

Jesse Marks paced back and forth impatiently. Keogh came to him and said, "Easy. We'll get 'em. The trail isn't but an hour old."

Jesse said, "I keep wondering what they'll look like. They ought to look like monsters, considering what they did, but I'll bet they don't. I'll bet they look like the kind of men you see every day."

"Likely. They're probably drifters, going from place to place. They're stupid or they wouldn't have done what they did. They've got no consciences. If we don't get them, they'll kill again and again."

Jesse Marks voiced his first doubts. "What if the court lets them off? What if Sarah's word isn't good enough to satisfy the judge?"

Keogh said, "They wouldn't get out of town alive if the judge let them go."

"Then why bother with a trial? If they're dead no matter what, why bother with a trial at all?"

Keogh looked at him strangely, but he didn't answer hast-

ily and he didn't come up with the obvious. Finally he said,
"Because of what it would do to the men who did the lynching.
A jury can find men guilty and a judge can sentence them
and everybody feels like they were just doing their civic duty.
They might feel bad for a while but they don't feel guilty. A
lynching is something else. There's always doubt that the men
lynched were guilty of what they were supposed to have done.
There's no pretense that what's being done is lawful because
everybody knows it's not." He walked to his horse and began
to saddle up. Jesse followed suit and so did the other men.
Keogh led out, with Jesse following and the others coming
along behind.

The terrain grew rougher all day as they climbed toward
the higher peaks twenty-five miles away. Going was slow.
The trail stayed clear of the roads, which mostly ran along
the banks of creeks or in dry drainages. It was up and down
hills all the way, and sometimes tracking was difficult because
of either rocky ground or a deep covering of pine needles in
forested areas.

The sun sank slowly toward the snow-capped mountains
to the west. The air was cooler now, at this higher altitude.
Finally Keogh ordered the rest of the posse to drop back a
quarter mile, and began scouting the ridges before letting
himself and his horse be skylined on them. Near sundown, he
beckoned Jesse, who was a couple of hundred yards behind.
Jesse left his horse and crawled up beside the sheriff.

The pair they were pursuing had camped in the draw
ahead. There was a trickle of water in it, and a grove of
scrubby trees. Their horses had been unsaddled and were
picketed a few hundred yards away, where there was a small
expanse of grass.

Keogh said, "You keep half of the posse here, but keep 'em
back out of sight. I'll take the rest and circle around. See that
big pine on the ridge over there? I'll give you a wave from

there, and we'll all come down on them at once. If they try to go either upstream or down, we can cut 'em off."

Jesse nodded. Both he and the sheriff eased back far enough to stand up without being seen. Then they returned to where the posse was waiting. Keogh gave his instructions quickly. Half the men followed him off to the right. Jesse remained with the others. He gave the sheriff fifteen minutes before stealthily returning to the crest of the ridge.

The sun was down now, and its dying rays stained the clouds overhead a brilliant copper red. It faded gradually. The clouds had turned salmon pink when Jesse saw the sheriff appear beside the pines on the other side of the ravine.

Standing, he beckoned to the dozen or so posse members behind him in the draw. They mounted and came up the slope, one of them leading Jesse's horse. Jesse took the reins, mounted, and led the way down toward the camp below. On the opposite slope the sheriff led his men down, having spread them out into a line a couple of hundred yards long. Jesse motioned to the men behind him to spread out similarly.

The two men spotted them while they were still a hundred and fifty yards away. Both sprinted instantly for their horses, but stopped when Jesse's men broke into a gallop and they saw that they weren't going to make it in time. They hesitated about drawing their guns, then decided against it. Closer than Keogh, Jesse Marks called sharply, "Shuck the gunbelts. Play it smart, boys. You haven't got a chance."

Carefully, the two men unbuckled their gunbelts and let them fall. Jesse called, "Now get back to camp."

The men followed his orders. They stopped beside their camp fire. Jesse and his men dismounted. So did Keogh and those with him. The posse surrounded the two men, one of whom asked plaintively, "What the hell's this all about? We ain't done nothing."

Jesse's anger was rising rapidly but he managed to keep his voice calm. He said, "We trailed you. From where you raped that girl. From where you threw her and her sister off the cliff."

Both men's faces were gray now and sweat gave their skin a shine in the dying light. Both swallowed and one blurted, "That's a lie, mister. We never touched no girls." Both looked as if they were going to bolt, but neither made a move.

Jesse walked closer to the men. He had been right when he'd told Keogh that they would probably look like men they saw every day. One was about five feet ten, stocky and strong-looking. The other was shorter and wiry. Both had several days' growth of whiskers. Both were weathered and dark. Both wore ragged range clothes and both were dirty, the way men get traveling in a country that is mostly dry.

Keogh, approaching from behind the men, made them turn their heads. As the larger of the two turned his, Jesse saw scratches on his neck. There were three, about two inches long, and parallel. They were the kind of scratches that would be made by a struggling girl's fingernails.

Suddenly Jesse's anger boiled over. In his mind he saw this man struggling with Sarah on the ground, she fighting with all her strength, he tearing at her clothes. He let out a sound that was half a cry of anguish, half a roar of rage. Like a grizzly bear, he charged.

He bowled the man back, knocking him down, falling himself. He lunged to his feet and stumbled forward. He put a knee in the man's belly as he came down, and almost simultaneously his hands closed on the man's throat.

There was a stink to this one, sour and rancid, and it increased Jesse's anger and disgust. His fingers dug in, collapsing the man's windpipe, cutting off air from his lungs. The man began to kick and thrash in furious desperation. His hands and fingers groped frantically for Jesse's eyes.

Jesse turned his head back and forth, avoiding them. His fingers clamped down tighter and tighter. In his ears was a roar, the sound of many voices, angry voices, all shouting. Hands were tugging at him, trying to pull him off. They only succeeded in dragging both him and his intended victim half a dozen feet along the ground.

Suddenly something solid slammed against the side of Jesse's head. Lights flashed before his eyes. His hands relaxed and the man beneath him fought clear. Jesse was helplessly rolled aside. He wasn't unconscious but, for the moment, he couldn't move nor understand what was happening. The roaring was still in his ears. Nearer, he heard the shouting voice of a single man. A gunshot split the night. Through the mist before his eyes Jesse glimpsed a scene that tipped wildly back and forth, a scene that contained the struggling forms of many men.

He shook his head, partially clearing it. He came to his hands and knees. Raising his head, he saw Keogh facing the members of the posse, his shotgun in his hands, smoke curling from the muzzle. And suddenly the roaring sound of voices stopped.

Jesse's vision was clearing fast. It was dusk now, but there was enough light to see the posse members and each of the two drifters being held by at least half a dozen men. The drifters' clothes were torn, their hats gone. Both were bleeding from nose and mouth. One was bent almost double, his face contorted with pain. Jesse pushed himself unsteadily to his feet. He remembered now. He had attacked the man with the scratches on his neck. He'd been choking him. Keogh must have tried to pull him off. Failing, he had clipped Jesse with his gun.

Gingerly, Jesse felt the side of his head where a bump was already rising fast. The sheriff said harshly, "The next charge goes right into the middle of you! Damn it, nobody's going to

lynch my prisoners! These men are going back to Pawnee
Bluffs and get a proper trial!"

Frank Fothergill was a horse trader who made his home in
Pawnee Bluffs. He was tall, whip thin, with hair and mustache
that were almost white. He drank a lot and spent most of his
time in the saloon. He was admired by most of the men in
town, perhaps because many of them secretly wished they
could live the way he did. Now, Fothergill assumed the leader-
ship of the men. He yelled, "Oh no! We know they did it because we trailed them from the place it happened! If we take
'em back to Pawnee Bluffs, it will tear the town apart and you
know it will. Best thing is to get rid of them here and take their
bodies back."

The men of the posse roared approval. Somebody shouted,
"Get some ropes!"

Jesse glanced at the sheriff's face. It was grim and taut,
but there was a flicker of indecision in the sheriff's eyes. Jesse
wondered if the men had seen it, and knew that if they had,
they would have their way.

Suddenly he realized that he had started this. If he hadn't
attacked one of the men the posse would never have gotten
out of control. It was up to him to set things right.

He dropped a hand to the gun at his side, hoping that it
had not fallen from the holster during the struggle on the
ground. Relief washed over him as his hand closed on its
grips. He pulled it out and thumbed the hammer. In the noise
the click of the hammer being cocked could not be heard, but
Jesse's shout could. "Fothergill, if we have a lynching here,
you won't see it because you're going to be the first to die." He
raised the gun to eye level. Holding it with both hands so that
it would be absolutely steady, he aimed it at Fothergill's chest.

Out of the corner of his eye, he saw Keogh glance at him.
He hoped the sheriff's indecision was gone. It must have been
because it wasn't apparent in Keogh's voice as he yelled, "He

means it, Fothergill! Now, all of you, release those men! We'll tie them up for the night and tomorrow we'll take them back to Pawnee Bluffs!"

Fothergill stared at the muzzle of Jesse's gun. His face had lost color and his eyes were scared. In a voice filled with outrage he said, "For Christ's sake, Jesse, it was your girl he . . ."

Jesse's gun didn't waver. He said, "Do what the sheriff says."

He didn't know how long the silence lasted. It seemed like five minutes but could not have been more than a minute or so. His arms began to tire from holding the revolver so rigidly.

Then Fothergill folded. He said, "Oh, hell, them two ain't worth any of us getting killed. Let's do what they say, boys. We can hang 'em when we get back to town."

Jesse didn't lower his gun, nor did the sheriff relax his vigilance. The two men were released and the sheriff said, "Over here, you two."

The two men came forward. They got behind the sheriff and stood there, faces gray, knees shaking visibly. Jesse slowly lowered his gun but did not put it away immediately.

Keogh called out four names. "Come tie them up. Then let's get some fires built and eat."

The four men came forward sullenly. They ordered the two to sit with their backs to a couple of scrub trees and began to tie them.

Suddenly the tension was gone. Keogh looked at Jesse, the shadow of a shaky grin on his face. Jesse shoved his gun into its holster and went to look for firewood, wondering if what he'd done was right. He supposed that only time would tell.

CHAPTER 5

Sheriff Keogh stood with his back to the fire and watched the two killers being tied. He knew that there was no doubt of their guilt. He and Jesse had trailed them from where they had raped Sarah. She would identify them as the pair that had attacked her and thrown her off the cliff. They would be tried, found guilty, sentenced to death, and hanged. It would be over with.

The men tying the ropes were pulling on them savagely and every now and then one of the prisoners would cry out with pain, which seemed to give pleasure to those tying them. Keogh didn't intervene because he understood how the four posse members felt. He felt the same way himself. He wanted to see the prisoners hurt. What they had done to the two helpless girls had been incredibly brutal. He had kept them from being hanged but that was as far as he was going to go.

The other men were silently gathering wood. Several additional fires were built. Horses were unsaddled and picketed up and down the narrow stream wherever there was grass. The panniers from the packhorse were unpacked and the men got out the food. Some began to cook and after a while the air turned strong with the smell of frying meat.

Jesse returned. He got a frypan from the pack, filled it with bacon, and put it on to cook. He also got a coffeepot, filled it with water, and put it beside the frypan to heat. Keogh continued to stare gloomily at the prisoners.

A premonition was bothering him. It made him uneasy and uncomfortable.

The four tying the prisoners finished the job, angrily pulling tight the last knots in the ropes. One of them, Ernie Simons, kicked his man before he walked away. Keogh didn't say anything. The prisoner grunted but did not cry out.

Jesse finished the bacon and put some cold biscuits into the grease to fry. By the time they were brown, the coffee was done. Keogh hunkered down beside the fire, filled a plate, and began to eat. Jesse followed suit.

Jesse said doubtfully, "I wish I was sure what we did was right."

"Don't worry, it was right."

Jesse was silent for several minutes. Finally he said, "We're not going to stop Reuben Lillard as easy as we did these men."

"I know it."

Jesse was studying his face. "Would you have pulled the trigger?"

Keogh turned his head. He grinned ruefully. He didn't honestly know whether or not he would have fired the shotgun. Then his grin faded. There wasn't anything in the least bit funny about what was happening. And this was only the beginning. He said, "I don't know. How the hell does anybody know what they're going to do until the time actually comes? Maybe if they'd rushed us, I'd have pulled the trigger. Would you have killed Fothergill?"

"Yes, sir. I'd have killed him."

"You're sure?"

"I'm sure. But that's some different than firing a shotgun into a crowd of men. Particularly from that distance."

Keogh was surprised. He continued to watch Jesse, glad he had him for a deputy. Admittedly, Jesse had precipitated the trouble a little while ago by his attack on the larger of the two prisoners, but Keogh was pretty sure that that wouldn't be repeated. Jesse wouldn't lose control of himself again.

One of the prisoners called, "Sheriff?"

Keogh glanced toward the man. "What?"

"How about us? Ain't we going to get anything to eat?"

Keogh glanced toward the nearest group of possemen. All of them were staring challengingly at him. All were scowling, as if daring him to give the prisoners anything. Keogh got up. He walked to the prisoners and Jesse followed him. Speaking so that he would not be overheard, he said, "If I was you, I'd keep my mouth shut until I was safe in jail. We kept you from being lynched once. That don't mean we can do it a second time."

"All we want is something to eat."

"All right, go ahead. Yell your damn head off, but don't expect any help from me if they put a rope around your neck."

The man grumbled, but he didn't call out and Keogh knew that he would not. He asked, "What's your names?"

The bigger of the two men said, "Bert Johnson. My side-kick's name is Schwartz."

"Those your real names?"

"Sure they are. We ain't outlaws, mister. We was just lookin' for work."

"Where you from?"

Jesse stalked away, his face red, his fists clenched. He went back to the fire and stared moodily into the flames. Stooping, he poured himself half a cup of lukewarm coffee. He could hear Keogh's voice, and that of Johnson, but couldn't understand their words.

He was going to have to stay away from those two as much as he could. Every time he got close to them he thought about what they'd done and he got mad. He wanted them dead. He wanted to kill them himself. Instead of being able to, he had to defend them—with his life, if it became necessary. Sourly he kicked a stick, the end of which was in the fire, and it scattered a shower of sparks for ten or fifteen feet. The men nearest him studied him and finally looked away.

Keogh returned. He turned his head toward the possemen and called, "You'd just as well get some sleep. We'll be traveling at dawn."

"What about them?" asked Fothergill.

"They'll be all right. They're tied. Either Jesse or me will be on watch all night."

"So they don't get away or so nothin' happens to them?"

"Both. Go ahead. Get some sleep."

Jesse said, "I'll take the first watch if you want me to."

"All right. Call me when you get tired." Keogh went to his saddle and untied his blanket roll. He spread the canvas on the ground near the fire, lay down, fully dressed, and pulled the blankets over him. His revolver dug into his hip, so he pulled it out of the holster and laid it beside him on the ground.

He didn't move, and after about five minutes he began to snore. Jesse stared at him with open amazement. Incredible as it seemed, Keogh could sleep whenever he lay down and closed his eyes. No matter what the strain.

Jesse himself walked to the prisoners and stared coldly down at them. Johnson said, "I don't suppose it would do any good to ask you to loosen up these ropes."

"No, it wouldn't."

Johnson stared resentfully at him, tried to hold his glance and failed. Jesse found himself a seat on the trunk of a fallen tree. He sat down, pulled his sack of Bull Durham from his pocket, and rolled a cigarette. He lighted it, aware that the smoke drifted to the prisoners. Johnson looked at him as if he were about to speak, then changed his mind.

The posse members were busy spreading their beds, settling into them. Jesse got up and began pacing back and forth.

He couldn't get Sarah out of his mind. He couldn't forget what had happened to her. He couldn't get over his shock that two such men even existed on the face of the earth. He felt himself getting hot with anger again and forced himself to think of something else.

It wasn't easy. The more he tried to guide his thoughts into other channels the more they came back to where they had begun. Finally he walked away into the darkness. He found himself a spot from which he could see the area between the sleeping posse members and the prisoners but could not actually see the prisoners themselves.

Now he thought of Sarah, the way she had been before this had happened to her. She was a spirited girl with a mind of her own. She probably got that from her father, Jesse thought. Her sweet disposition must have come from her mother.

His eye caught movement against the light of the dying fires. He broke into a run, charging back toward the two trussed prisoners.

Fothergill stood behind the prisoners. He held a rifle in both hands, raised, poised in such a way that he could bring the heavy butt down against Johnson's head. Jesse said sharply, "Fothergill!"

The man turned his head and glanced at Jesse. Jesse couldn't see his face because of the shadow lying over it. But none of the tension went out of the tall, slim man and Jesse said, more softly, "Do it and I'll kill you."

Fothergill said, "You wouldn't."

Jesse was irritated at having twice been put into the position of defending the men who had abused Sarah and killed her sister. His irritation was plain in his voice. "Try me then!"

Fothergill stood there motionlessly for what seemed like an eternity. Finally he lowered the gun and took a step away from the prisoners. Jesse approached him. Fothergill faced him, the rifle held in front of him in both his hands. His face, illuminated now by the dim light from the fires, was filled with defiance.

Jesse didn't draw his gun. He waited until he was only a step away from Fothergill and then he moved. He seized Fothergill's rifle and yanked it toward him.

Fothergill did not release it. He tried to pull it back. Using that force and his own strength to force the gun upward, Jesse slammed it against the tall horse trader's throat.

Fothergill fell back. He released the gun and clawed at his throat. He choked, and his face turned dark as he tried frantically to draw air into his lungs. He began to writhe on the ground in terror, afraid he would never breathe again.

Jesse knelt. He unbuckled Fothergill's belt and yanked it clear. Pulling the man's hands around behind him, he tied them swiftly and securely with the belt.

The sheriff was awake. He didn't get up; he didn't even sit up. He only watched as Jesse got rope and tied Fothergill's feet.

By now Fothergill was breathing again, in great, hoarse gasps. Jesse went to where Fothergill had been sleeping. He got the man's blankets, gathered them up, and brought them back. He covered Fothergill angrily.

Fothergill said, "You ain't going to leave me like this, are you?"

"I am. You've made enough trouble for one night."

"Sheriff . . ." Fothergill glanced at Keogh, lying twenty feet away.

Keogh said, "Shut up and go to sleep. You're lucky Jesse

caught you before you killed that man. Otherwise you'd be charged with murder, too."

Fothergill started to say something, then changed his mind. Jesse didn't leave again. He sat down on the fallen tree and stared at the ground between his feet.

CHAPTER 6

Jesse didn't call the sheriff until well after midnight. The prisoners were still awake when he did so, but he suspected that they had dozed off occasionally. Keogh got up and Jesse lay down and pulled his blanket over him. The fires had all died to beds of coals that glowed only occasionally when the breeze blew on them.

Jesse closed his eyes. He hadn't thought he would be able to sleep, but he was too exhausted to stay awake. He fell asleep almost as quickly as the sheriff had.

It seemed only an instant before the sheriff shook him awake. The sky in the east was turning gray. Men were moving around, feeding the fires and restarting them.

Jesse got up. He glanced toward the prisoners. Keogh said, "We'll wait until there's something for them to eat. Then we'll let them loose."

Jesse walked away from camp. When he came back he had an armload of wood. He dumped it beside the fire and busied himself cooking something for the four of them to eat. He knew it would be useless to ask anybody else to cook for the prisoners.

When the food was finished Keogh untied the prisoners. He had to help them to their feet, one at a time, and steady them until enough circulation had returned to enable them to stand. For a while they hobbled back and forth, in obvious pain. Finally they came to the fire, where they helped themselves to food.

Both Jesse and Keogh were finished long before the prisoners. Each saddled two horses. Jesse cleaned the dishes and pots and repacked them. It was light when the posse rode out, heading back toward Pawnee Bluffs.

There was no trouble with the members of the posse today. Mostly the men were silent, riding along almost glumly, having accepted the idea that the prisoners were going to be returned to town alive. That didn't mean, Jesse knew, that they had accepted the idea of peacefully letting the men come to trial. First thing most of them would do when they hit town would be to head for the saloon. They'd start drinking, along with all the men who had stayed behind, and by the time it got dark they'd be ready for another try at taking the prisoners out and hanging them.

He wasn't prepared for what did happen when they rode into town in mid-afternoon. He and Keogh were in the lead, the two prisoners following. The posse was strung out behind for several hundred yards.

Everybody in town seemed to be gathered in the middle of Bluff, the main business street. When Jesse and Keogh rode into sight, a sound went up from the gathered throng. It wasn't a roar, exactly. Just a rumbling sound. Jesse knew that they had been seen coming down the road out of the hills in time for word to get around.

He still wasn't ready for what happened as they began pushing their way through the edges of the crowd. People he had known for years began yelling at him like maniacs. Hands seized the legs of the prisoners. When the men tried to kick them away, it only further enraged the crowd.

Women screamed, "Hang them! Kill them!" Keogh looked at Jesse. He didn't have to say anything. Jesse knew what the look meant and what Keogh wanted him to do. He spurred his horse, forcing the frightened, trembling animal forward through the screaming throng. People were knocked down, and got up angrier than they had been before. It was bedlam. Neither Jesse nor the sheriff was able to understand all the things being yelled at them. But the gist was plain enough: this mob wanted the prisoners and was willing to do whatever was necessary to get them.

A rock struck Jesse on the head, knocking off his hat, stunning him momentarily. More rocks were thrown, some striking the horse. The animal reared, nickering shrilly with terror. Jesse tried to bring him down where his hoofs wouldn't strike anybody.

They had come almost to a standstill. A solid wall of people barred their way. There were only two hundred and fifty people in Pawnee Bluffs, but it looked as if all of them were here. There were even children in the crowd.

A rock struck the sheriff and he roared with anger. He spurred his horse savagely and the animal plunged ahead, past Jesse, bowling people to the right and left, forcing a way through and leaving a path behind. Jesse put his horse into it and the prisoners followed, white-faced and thoroughly terrified.

A voice louder than the rest bawled, "Let's take 'em up and throw 'em over the cliff like they did the Lillard girls!"

Another shouted, "That's too damn good for them! Let's stretch their necks with a couple of ropes!"

Jesse looked over the heads of the angry mob. The jail was only half a block away but it looked like a mile. The crowd was pressing in now, trying to close off the passageway the sheriff's horse was making. Jesse kicked his horse ahead and got immediately behind the sheriff's horse.

A yell of pure terror made him turn his head. He was in time to see Johnson yanked bodily off his horse by half a dozen men. He hit the street and almost immediately disappeared as the crowd surged over him.

Jesse didn't have time to think. He left his horse, knocking down a man as he did. He plunged back toward the place where Johnson had disappeared.

They were beating Johnson with their fists, crowding, fighting each other for a chance to get in a lick on him. It was uncontrolled madness with a frenzy to it, the way there sometimes is when a man kills a rattlesnake. Jesse yanked away a man and crowded past him. He yanked away two more before he reached Johnson. He roared, "Stop it! Let him up! Goddamnit, you're killing him!"

There was a commotion behind him. There was the sudden roar of the sheriff's shotgun, a sound that, for an instant, froze everything and everyone. Jesse took immediate advantage of it. He stooped and yanked Johnson to his feet, and shoved him savagely toward his horse. Johnson managed to catch hold of the saddle horn but he couldn't mount. The mob was crowding close again, clawing at his clothes, trying to pull him loose.

Jesse pushed back toward his own animal. Fists, thrown wildly, struck him on the back and the side of the head. He didn't pull his gun because he still wasn't ready to kill anyone.

He was able to grab his horse's tail. Keogh, pushing his own horse ruthlessly back through the crowd, struck Jesse's animal on the rump with a quirt. The horse plunged forward, dragging Jesse along with him.

Keogh struck Johnson's horse the same way, and he came plunging after Jesse's animal. Johnson, still clinging desperately to the saddle horn, was dragged along.

The sheriff was using the quirt indiscriminately now. Jesse, without letting go of his horse's tail, glanced behind.

The quirt drove back people who would not have retreated for anything else. Keogh struck faces, shoulders, backs. He slashed a path to Schwartz's horse. He got behind the animal and cut him viciously across the rump. The horse lunged through the crowd, thinned by Keogh's quirt, and followed the other horses toward the jail. Keogh followed, quirting both Schwartz's horse and his own whenever somebody tried to stop them or bar their way.

Jesse reached the jail. He flung open the door. Johnson lunged through the doorway and turned to stand, white-faced and sweating, in the middle of the room. There was blood on his face. Out in front, Schwartz tumbled from his horse and came stumbling in. Keogh followed, leaving the horses loose out front.

To Jesse it seemed like a nightmare, something impossible that nevertheless was happening. Women and children were weeping in the street, those, he supposed, who had been hurt in the melee. Men shouted angry threats, curses, and obscenities. Keogh slammed the door and bolted it. Immediately rocks began striking it. One shattered the window on the right side of the door and broken glass cascaded to the floor.

In a voice calmer than Jesse would have thought possible, Keogh said, "Lock 'em up."

Jesse looked at the two prisoners. They were as terrified as a bird cornered by a snake. He said, "All right. Go on out back."

Neither of the prisoners moved. They were staring with fascination at the door. Jesse nudged them, startled to discover that he didn't want to kill them anymore. Killing would be too easy. Lynching would be too easy. This way, they were suffering the same helpless terror they had put into Sarah and Melissa before throwing them off the cliff.

Like sleepwalkers the men stumbled toward the door leading to the cells. Jesse pushed them into one, then closed and locked the door. A rock smashed the cell window as he did. The two men hurriedly crossed the cell and cringed against the wall.

Jesse went back into the office. The sheriff was reloading

his double-barreled ten-gauge. Jesse said, "Jesus, I never saw anything like that in my life!"

"You'd better hope you never see it again."

"What are we going to do?"

"Hold the jail and hope they cool off after a while."

"What if they don't?"

Keogh shrugged. The rocks had stopped pelting the jail. It was not quite so noisy in the street. Most of the women had either stopped weeping or gone home. The men had either run out of curses and epithets or gone into the saloon.

Jesse approached the window cautiously. He was shocked and appalled at the change he had seen in these people he knew so well. They had been like animals, their faces contorted, their mouths twisted into ugly shapes. Their friendship and respect for the sheriff and Jesse had disappeared before their lust for the two killers' blood. Jesse realized with horror that they would have killed Keogh and himself if that had been the only way to get the prisoners. All that had prevented it had been the sheriff's ruthlessness in forcing a path through them.

Only a few now stood in the street, staring at the jail. Their faces seemed drained of emotion. They stared blankly, as if they didn't know what to do. Jesse turned away.

He started violently as someone began banging on the door, apparently with the barrel of a gun. Keogh yelled, "Who is it?"

"Lillard. Open this goddamn door!"

"Anybody with you?"

"Galen Sauls."

"That all?"

"Yes, that's all! Now open up!"

Keogh pointed the shotgun at the door, his thumb on the right-hand hammer. He said, "All right. Unlock it and then get to one side."

Jesse pulled back the bolt and stepped quickly to the side. Keogh called, "It's open! Come on in!"

The door slammed open and Reuben Lillard stepped angrily into the room. Galen Sauls, his foreman, came in immediately behind. Both men wore guns, but neither had a gun in his hand. Lillard said, "I want to see them! I want to see what kind of dirty animals do a thing like that!"

Keogh said, "Shuck your guns."

Surprisingly, Lillard did not protest. He unbuckled his gunbelt and laid it on the desk. Sauls followed suit. Keogh said, "I've got to search you."

Neither man protested, which was as surprising to Jesse as their giving up their guns. Keogh searched them quickly. He nodded toward the door leading to the cells. "All right. Go take a look. Jesse, go with them."

Jesse opened the door and held it for Lillard and Sauls. Keogh closed and bolted the front door. Jesse followed the two men into the corridor between the two rows of cells.

Lillard just stood at the bars and stared. His hands, each clutching a bar, were knuckle-white and his arms were trembling. Jesse stared at his ashen face, at his blazing eyes, at his thinly compressed mouth. He didn't like Lillard and never had, even before Lillard had ordered Sarah to stop seeing him. But he knew exactly how Lillard felt. He'd felt that way himself when they'd first caught up with the two fugitives. Only there hadn't been any bars between him and the pair.

Lillard released the bars. He turned, put his blazing glance on Jesse for an instant, then stalked back into the office. Sauls followed. Jesse closed the door and stood with his back to it.

Lillard looked at Keogh. "I want them, Morg. I'm not going to have this go to trial. I'm not going to let my girl get up in front of everybody and have to say what they done to her."

Keogh said, "I'm sorry, Reuben. I can't give them to you."

Jesse glanced at Lillard's hands. They hung at his sides and were clenched as tightly as they had been a few minutes ago, holding on to the bars.

Lillard said, "I'm not asking you, Morg. I'm telling you. Give them to me or take the consequences."

Keogh shook his head. He withdrew the guns from the holsters on the desk and ejected the cartridges from them. He replaced them in their holsters and held them out to Lillard and Galen Sauls. He said, "Give yourselves time to cool off."

Lillard snatched his gun and belt from the sheriff's hands. Sauls took his more quietly. At the closed door, Lillard turned. His glance seemed to scorch everything it touched. Without another word he opened the door and stepped outside. Jesse hurriedly crossed the room, closed the door and bolted it.

CHAPTER 7

Jesse stood with his back to the bolted door, leaning on it, suddenly drained. He said wearily, "They'll be back."

Keogh nodded.

"So will the townspeople."

Keogh nodded again. "Want to quit?"

"You know better than that. But what are you going to do when they all come back? Those two aren't worth killing anybody over."

"The law is."

Jesse Marks stared at him.

Keogh said, "I told you before. I've seen what a lynching does to a town—to the people that live in it. I'm not going to let it happen here. No matter what I have to do."

"What about Lillard?"

"What about him?"

Jesse Marks suddenly was confused and didn't know what to say. There was something between the sheriff and Reuben Lillard, something personal. He sensed it, and it changed things.

Keogh let him off the hook. He said, "Maybe you're right. Maybe it would be harder with Lillard than with anybody else."

"Why?"

Keogh hesitated for a moment, then shrugged. "Lillard and me go back a long time. Twenty-five, maybe thirty years."

Marks crossed the room and sat down on the narrow cot.

Keogh said, "When Lillard and me came here, there wasn't anything. No town. Nothing. I was driving a freight wagon and I picked this place to break my leg. There was a road house down close to the creek and I laid up there, waiting for it to heal. Lillard already had a couple of hundred cattle here, and a log shack back up in the hills."

Jesse Marks waited for him to continue. Thoughtfully, Keogh packed his pipe and lighted it. Finally he went on, "I went to work for Lillard when my leg got well. Worked for him about three years. By then a town had started here. There were other ranches over in the hills besides Lillard's. Drifters coming through, and wagon trains. People wanted a town and a county, and that meant law. They hired me."

He puffed on his pipe for several moments. "Reuben and me were friends. Until Amanda came. Her pa had died of typhoid a hundred miles east of here. She couldn't drive over the mountains and the wagon train didn't have an extra man to drive for her. So she stayed. Lillard and me both started courting her. Courted her for the best part of a year. I guess it must've been about the same week that Lillard and me both asked. She said yes to me. That was the end of me and Lillard being friends. Amanda and I were married and I had a house built for us. That little one down there about two blocks this side of the creek. We moved in before it was hardly finished." He frowned, even now, after twenty-five years, remembering hurt. Finally he said, "We had almost a year. Then one day we were walking up Bluff Street together. It happened right there in front of Waite's Mercantile. The bank was in the back of the store those days. Couple of drifters came running out, carrying a bag and waving guns. I pushed Amanda back and told her to run. I hollered at the men to throw down their guns. Only Amanda didn't run. She just stood there, scared for me, I guess. The robbers commenced shooting at me and me at them. When it was over, they was both dead and so was Amanda. She'd caught a bullet meant for me."

Marks, watching the sheriff's eyes, saw the pain in them. He said uneasily, "Don't talk about it if you don't want to."

"It's all right. I haven't ever talked about it before. Seeing what happened to Sarah, I reckon you know how I felt. Lillard—well, he blamed me. Said if I hadn't been wearing a badge it wouldn't have happened. He said if Amanda had married him instead of me, she'd still be alive and it was true."

Marks was beginning to understand why Keogh had told about his wife and her death. It explained Lillard's angry opposition to Sarah marrying him. He didn't want her married to a lawman, no matter who he was.

He asked, "Then you think that's why he didn't want Sarah seeing me?"

"What else?" Keogh grinned faintly at him. "You're not exactly a prize, but you're not as bad as Lillard makes you out to be."

Jesse Marks felt better to realize it wasn't personal with Lillard. At least not entirely. But it didn't change anything. If he and Sarah were married, it would have to be without her father's consent.

Keogh was watching him. "What about what's happened? You still want to marry her?"

Marks stared at the sheriff. "Sure I do. Why wouldn't I want to marry her? What's changed?"

Keogh's face darkened with embarrassment. He mumbled, "I shouldn't have mentioned it."

"Shouldn't have mentioned what?"

Keogh's mouth firmed out. He said, "Well, some men would think things had changed. Sarah was raped by both those men. It's going to change things some even if you give her lots of time." Keogh was thoroughly embarrassed now and his expression said that he wished he'd never brought up the subject.

But Marks understood what he was getting at. Sarah wouldn't be able to help comparisons between the marriage relationship and the rape. He muttered, "We'll work it out."

"Sure you will." Keogh busied himself relighting his pipe. Marks was relieved that the discussion was finished.

At the same time he was glad that the sheriff had mentioned it, even if it had been embarrassing for both of them. He hadn't considered the difficulties, except for the obvious, that Sarah was going to feel soiled and only his own steadfast devotion would get her over it.

He wanted to see her. He almost asked if he could leave, then changed his mind. Right now Keogh needed him. If the town calmed down later on, then maybe he could go. He got up and nervously walked to the window and stared outside, an anxious frown on his face.

Reuben Lillard was used to having his own way. Back in the mountains west of town, he claimed and held an area roughly twenty miles long and five miles wide although he owned outright only the hundred-sixty-acre homestead claim the house sat on.

Fifteen men worked for him and his word was law. When he came to town, people treated him with deference and respect. His account in the bank ran to five figures and he didn't owe anything.

He sat at a table in the corner of the saloon. Galen Sauls sat across from him, silent, companionable, ready to do anything Lillard asked of him. The saloon was nearly full. Men stood solid at the bar and behind them stood others, waiting their turn.

A good many of these men had dust on them from the street. Some had bruises and some had cuts. All were angry, but for now they needed time to catch their breaths. The brawl in the street had been so violent that it had left most of them numb. Some, not many, were shocked at what they had tried to do, but most of those who felt this way had already gone home.

Sauls glanced at Lillard. "What now, boss?"

Lillard frowned. He seemed to be considering his next move for the first time. Still undecided, he grumbled, "I haven't changed my mind, if that's what you mean. Sarah's been through enough without havin' to go to court and tell what them two bastards did to her."

Sauls waited. He was loyal and would do what he was told, but he didn't necessarily have to approve of it. He happened to be one of those who had been shocked by the violence in the street. He had no sympathy for the two men who had killed Melissa and tried to kill Sarah, but he didn't like the things he had seen in the faces of all the people he'd thought he knew so well.

He poured himself a drink. Lillard's glass still sat in front of him, untouched. Sauls thought that Lillard, at least, wasn't feeding his hatred with alcohol.

When Lillard didn't speak, Sauls said, "Keogh won't let you have them, boss. You'll have to kill him before you get your hands on them." He waited an instant, then added, "And you'll have to kill Jesse Marks." He threw that in deliberately. He wanted Lillard to realize what people would say after it was over with: that he had killed Keogh because of something that had happened twenty-five years ago; that he had killed Jesse Marks to keep him from marrying Sarah. Sauls and Lillard might know it wasn't true, but Lillard ought to realize now how things would look.

Lillard glared at him. Sauls met the angry glance steadily. Finally Lillard said, "Maybe not. There ought to be some way of getting the prisoners without killing Keogh and Marks."

Sauls shrugged and finished his drink. He didn't know of any way, and even if he had, he didn't want any part in it.

Almost as if speaking to himself, Lillard said, "God, if only Sarah and me hadn't had that fight!" Suddenly he picked up his drink, downed it, poured another, and drank that, too. He looked at Sauls, intense pain in his eyes. "God, they must have hit every damn rock all the way to the bottom. If I hadn't known it was Melissa, I'd never have recognized her. Her face . . ." He covered his own face with his hands. He sat there rigidly for a long time. Sauls filled his glass for him. If Lillard could drink enough, he thought, maybe he'd be able to go to sleep. Sleep would not only ease his misery, it would get him off the streets for the night. Without Lillard to push things, maybe Keogh could keep the lid on the town. And by tomorrow maybe people would have cooled off.

Sauls said, "Drink up, boss. There's no use torturin' yourself."

Lillard drank, making a face afterward. He asked, "What time is it?"

Sauls glanced at the clock behind the bar. It was early, not yet five o'clock. He said, "Almost five. Why don't you go over and get a room at the hotel. Get yourself a few hours' sleep. You was up most of last night, wasn't you?"

"I dozed off once in a while over at Doc's."

"Anything you want me to do?"

Lillard shook his head.

"Want me to go get you a room?"

Again Lillard shook his head. "I couldn't sleep. I'd just lay there and see Sarah the way she looked when we found her. I'd see Melissa the way she looked when they brought her in."

Sauls shrugged. Maybe it *would* be better if Lillard waited until later to go to bed. If he went now he might wake up at nine or ten o'clock, sick and angry again and wanting to hang the two men and have it over with.

Sauls poured himself another drink. He tried to relax, but there was a tension in him that wouldn't go away. Terrible things had happened, but other terrible things were going to happen before all this was over with. He knew it in his bones.

CHAPTER 8

At six o'clock Keogh got up, went to the window, and stared outside. The street, at the supper hour, was nearly deserted, even though the Pawnee Saloon, up the street, appeared to be almost full. Keogh turned his head and looked at Jesse Marks. "It's quiet and it'll stay that way until after supper. Why don't you go on up and see Sarah while her old man is in the saloon. When you get back, I'll see about some food for us and the prisoners."

Jesse got up from the cot. He desperately wanted to see Sarah, but he was worried. What if she refused to see him? What if she told him she never wanted to see him again?

But why should she? He was in no way responsible for what had happened, even if the fight with her father had been over him.

He went to the door almost reluctantly. He stepped outside and closed it, hearing the bolt slide as Keogh locked the door behind him.

The Pawnee Saloon was one of two saloons in Pawnee Bluffs. It was up the street half a block from the jail, and adjoined the Pawnee Hotel, though it was not a part of it. Downstreet, toward the bridge, was the Pink Lady Saloon. It, too, was open and seemed to be doing a thriving business. The Pawnee catered to the business and professional people in Pawnee Bluffs. The Pink Lady catered to those who worked with their hands and to the cowhands when they came to town on Saturday night. It was the larger of the two, and had rooms upstairs, where a cowboy could take one of the girls if he wanted to.

Marks hurried up the street. He cut between two buildings to the alley before he reached the Pawnee because he didn't want to take the chance of Lillard seeing him.

The sun was settling behind the high peaks to the west. It put a brief shine to the never-melting snow, then slid out of sight. Overhead, the clouds flamed orange and gold.

Doctor Peabody's house was a big, two-story frame at the upper end of Pine, a block off Bluff. Jesse stopped out front for a moment, hesitating, wondering if he ought to go in. Finally, squaring his shoulders unconsciously, he walked to the door, then turned the handle of the bell.

Mrs. Peabody came to the door. She was small, matronly, and had graying hair. She exclaimed, "Jesse Marks! You come right in! I'll bet you want to see Sarah, don't you?"

Jesse took off his hat and stepped inside. He said, "Yes, ma'am, if she's up to it."

"I'll call the doctor. You just sit down."

Jesse could smell meat frying in the kitchen. Mrs. Peabody left the room and Jesse sat down on the edge of a chair, his hat in his hands. Uneasily he looked around. Only then did he see Mrs. Lillard, sitting in a darkened corner by herself. He got up at once. "I didn't see you, Mrs. Lillard."

"It's all right, Jesse. Sit down."

Jesse perched on the edge of the chair again. He asked, "How is she, Mrs. Lillard?"

She looked small and helpless sitting there. She said, "Doctor Peabody says she is going to be all right. Why, I'll never know, after a fall like that. God must have been right beside her all the way, protecting her."

"Yes, ma'am."

"I understand you found Melissa. Thank you, Jesse." She began to cry.

"I'm sorry about her, ma'am. I'm awfully sorry." He felt helpless and inadequate. He wanted to comfort her and say something that had meaning but there wasn't anything to say.

"And I understand you caught the men who did those awful things."

"Well, ma'am, I was along. But they're in jail."

"Do you know where my husband is?"

"At the Pawnee, Mrs. Lillard. Along with Galen Sauls and some of the other men."

"He's taking it very hard. I hope . . ." She didn't finish, but Jesse thought he knew what she had been going to say.

Doctor Peabody came into the room, a slight man with a small paunch. His gray hair was thinning on top and he wore a pair of gold-rimmed spectacles. He said, "Hello, Jesse."

"Do you think . . . is Sarah well enough to see me now?"

"She's well enough, I think, but she's very upset. I'll ask her, if you like."

"Yes, sir. I'd appreciate it if you would."

Peabody hesitated for an instant. Jesse took the opportunity to ask, "Is she going to be all right?"

"Yes. She has no broken bones and the bruises and lacerations will heal. The state of her mind is something else. She has had a terrible experience."

"Yes, sir. I know she has."

Peabody turned toward the room where Sarah was, then turned back. He said, "Her face . . . well, it is badly bruised and swollen. I think it is important that you don't let her know if the sight of it is a shock to you."

"Yes, sir. I'll be careful."

Peabody went into the adjoining room and closed the door. Jesse could hear the deep cadence of his voice. Then he heard Sarah's voice and after that the doctor's voice again. When Sarah's voice came again, it was shriller and louder and fi-

nally hysterical. When she finally quieted the door opened
and the doctor came out again. He said, "I'm sorry, Jesse. She
doesn't want to see you now."

Jesse nodded numbly. He was hurt, but he supposed he
understood. Sarah's face was bruised and beaten and she
didn't want him to see it that way. Mrs. Lillard got up. "Let
me talk to her."

Peabody nodded. Jesse said, "It's all right, Mrs. Lillard.
I don't want her to do anything she doesn't want to do."

"Let me talk to her." Mrs. Lillard disappeared into Sarah's
room.

Jesse looked at Doc. Peabody said, "She doesn't know about
Melissa and I'd just as soon she didn't, at least for a while."

"Yes, sir. I won't mention her." He didn't really think that
Sarah was going to see him at all.

He could hear the murmur of voices behind the closed door
and suddenly he wished he hadn't come. He should have given
Sarah more time to get over what had happened to her. He
should have thought of her instead of himself, and stayed
away. But what if she'd wanted to see him and he had stayed
away? That would have been worse.

Peabody said hesitantly, "There's more to it than the way
she looks, Jesse. She has had a degrading experience. She
feels soiled. She may even feel that she is ruined."

Jesse Marks said indignantly, "It wasn't her fault! I don't
see why . . . !"

Peabody glanced at him approvingly. "Of course it wasn't
her fault. And she shouldn't feel the way she does. The point
is, she can't help herself. What she is feeling is what girls and
women have felt in like situations for centuries. She will probably get over it, given time."

Jesse Marks stared at him, outrage in his face. "What do
you mean *probably?* She's got to get over it!"

"I hope she will. She's healthy and strong and if she has you standing by . . ."

"Well, you don't have to worry about that!"

The door to Sarah's room opened and Mrs. Lillard came out. There were tears in her eyes. "She won't see you, Jesse. She says she never wants to see you again. But she'll get over it. Give her a little more time."

"Yes, ma'am." He tried not to show it, but he felt like he'd been kicked. Suddenly he wanted to get away. He didn't want to have to face these two people any longer. He couldn't stand the sympathetic looks they were giving him.

And his anger toward the two drifters was rekindled. He hurried to the door, opened it, and stepped outside.

Sarah's heart jumped when she heard Jesse's voice outside her room. She realized that she had been waiting to hear it and she felt tears of relief fill her eyes. She should have known that what had happened wouldn't change the way Jesse felt toward her. She should have known it would make no difference to him.

She raised her hands to fix her hair. Pain from the movement shot through her chest and both her arms. Instead of going to her hair, her hands went to her face, feeling the swelling that had nearly closed one of her eyes, feeling her bruised and puffy lips. She couldn't let Jesse see her looking like this. She hadn't been given a mirror but she knew she must look terrible.

Doctor Peabody came into the room and closed the door behind him. His eyes were kind. "Somebody here to see you, Sarah."

"Jesse?"

"Uh-huh."

"Where has he been? Why did it take him so long?"

"He's the sheriff's deputy, Sarah. He and Morgan Keogh took a posse and went after those two men."

"Did they get them?"

He nodded. "They have them down in jail."

Sarah winced. "Then he's talked to them. He knows what they did to me."

"He knew that before he left to track them down, Sarah."

"I don't want to see him."

"Why?" She had the feeling that Doctor Peabody knew, but he was going to force her to put it into words. She couldn't. She said, "I look awful. I don't want him to see me this way."

"I thought you and Jesse were going to be married."

"What's that got to do with it?"

"He won't care if your face is bruised."

"I don't want to see him," Sarah repeated stubbornly.

Peabody said, "Is it because of what those men did to you?"

"What if it is?"

"That won't make any difference either."

She stared at him. "You don't believe that and neither do I. It would make a difference to any man."

Peabody's glance held both sympathy and exasperation. Finally he said, "Why don't you let him come in and see for yourself?"

"No."

"Sarah, please. Give him a chance. Not only for him but for you. The sooner you start putting what happened out of your mind the sooner you're going to get over it."

Sarah could feel tears scalding her eyes. She could feel hysteria rising in her and couldn't control it. She heard herself screaming at Doctor Peabody. She screamed and screamed and couldn't stop.

Peabody didn't try to calm her but neither did he persist

in trying to get her to see Jesse Marks. Finally Sarah subsided, sobbing into her pillow. Peabody left the room.

Sarah wanted to see Jesse Marks. She felt abandoned and alone and more than anything else she wanted him to come in and comfort her and hold her in his arms. But she knew she couldn't let him. And she knew why. She was afraid . . . afraid of what she might see in his eyes.

The door opened and her mother came into the room. Sarah raised her head. Her mother said, "Jesse's here, Sarah."

"That's what Doctor Peabody said."

"He wants to see you. He feels so terrible about what happened to you and—" Her mother stopped suddenly.

"I don't want to see him now. I don't want him to see me looking like this."

"It won't make any difference to him."

"Won't it? What if it does, and what if I see it in his face?"

"You have to have faith in him."

"Maybe I can have faith later, Mama. I can't right now." Her mother nodded. "All right. I'll tell him."

Sarah's mother left the room. Sarah wished she had let Jesse come in, but knew she had been right in refusing him. Let him have a few days to adjust to what had happened, she told herself. Take a few days yourself to get to looking more normal, for the swelling to go down. Maybe then . . .

Someday, somehow, she was going to have to get up out of this bed and go out and face the people of the town, and Jesse, too. But she couldn't do it yet. She needed time to heal inside as well as out.

CHAPTER 9

Jesse stood for a moment on the porch of Doctor Peabody's house. The clouds had lost the color given them earlier by the setting sun and now were gray like the darkening sky.

The supper hour was over for most of the town's inhabitants, and they were beginning to come from their homes and head downtown. A couple of dogs barked monotonously.

Depressed and filled with uneasiness, Jesse stepped down off the porch and headed toward the jail. He heard pounding hoofbeats and saw the dim shapes of two horsemen a block away, approaching from the direction of downtown.

He stopped, staring curiously toward the approaching horsemen. Both pulled up, plunging, immediately beside him. Jesse recognized Reuben Lillard and his foreman, Galen Sauls.

Lillard was out of his saddle before the horse had stopped. He rushed toward Jesse, and when he was in range, released a haymaker that struck Jesse squarely on the nose. Stunned, Jesse staggered back. He tripped over an exposed tree root and went down. Lillard came after him, a sound like a snarl coming from his throat.

Blood streamed from Jesse's nostrils. He wiped his nose on a sleeve. Sauls caught Lillard and held him, both arms encircling him from behind. He yelled, "Boss, stop it!"

Lillard fought to be free, so furious that for the moment he couldn't speak. Sauls held on stubbornly, drawing a furious "Damn you, Sauls, let go of me!" from Lillard. Sauls said, "Calm down, boss. Beating on Jesse ain't going to help."

When Lillard spoke again his voice was under tight control. "I'm all right now. Let go of me."

"Boss . . ."

"Damn you, let go of me!" In his voice was a tone that made Sauls release him instantly. Lillard stepped away, shaking himself angrily.

Jesse was up now, his bandanna held to his streaming nose. It had taken all the self-control he could muster to keep from retaliating. He was still so angry that his head pounded and his face felt hot. He didn't know what would have happened if Sauls hadn't grabbed Lillard and held him until he'd calmed down. He'd have fought back, he supposed, and later would have regretted it because he didn't want any more trouble with Lillard than he already had.

Lillard's voice was not a shout, but it was loud enough to be heard for at least fifty yards. "Damn you, Marks, stay away from her! Stay away from her or I'll kill you with my own two hands!"

Jesse clenched his fists and controlled himself. It wasn't right for Sarah's father and him to be fighting here while she lay hurt not a hundred feet away. He just hoped Lillard's voice hadn't carried through an open window in Sarah's room. He made no reply, but his glance didn't waver from Lillard's furiously intemperate one.

Over Lillard's shoulder, Sauls stared at Jesse beseechingly, begging him to let it go. Jesse shrugged. He wasn't hurt. All he had was a bloody nose. And he had to admit that Lillard had a lot to be upset about. His youngest daughter lay dead at the undertaker's. His oldest daughter lay hurt in Doc Peabody's house. The men who had done it sat safely in a cell downtown, beyond his reach. He was simply taking his frustration out on Jesse because he was here.

Quite possibly he also blamed himself because it was a fight with him that had sent Sarah driving away so recklessly. And it was because of that fight that Melissa had followed her. Jesse turned away.

As he did, he saw someone standing on Doc Peabody's porch. It was too dark to definitely recognize Lillard's wife, but Jesse was sure it was she.

He slowly walked back toward the jail, leaving Lillard and Sauls talking. Lillard's voice was still angry, Sauls's stubbornly placating.

He wondered what it must have been like for Mrs. Lillard all these years, living with a man who cherished the memory of a woman he had lost even though she was dead. She must have felt that that woman was living in the same house with them, sitting at the table with them, sharing their bedroom at night.

He turned the corner. He took the bandanna away from his nose, relieved to discover that the bleeding had stopped. He'd have to have a clean shirt, he thought, and he'd have to wash off the blood. He detoured and went into the back door of the boarding house. He reached his room, poured some water into the basin, and shrugged out of his shirt.

He washed the blood off his face and hands, careful not to start his nose to bleeding again. He put on a clean shirt and tucked it in. He went out the door and down the back stairs. He walked along the alley in the direction of the jail.

His uneasiness returned. He knew what was causing it and he knew there was good reason for it. The town had only calmed temporarily. The people had gone home to supper but now they were coming back downtown. The saloons would fill up and there'd be a lot of drinking and talk. Eventually the talk would stop and they'd be like they'd been a while ago when he and Keogh had brought the prisoners in. They'd try to take them out of the jail by force.

A few people were standing across the street from the jail, silently staring at it. Noise came from the open doors of the Pawnee Saloon and from the Pink Lady, farther down. But the tinkle of pianos was missing. So was the sound of laughing, both women's and men's.

None of those watching the jail spoke to Jesse when he spoke to them. He knocked on the jail door and Keogh opened it. He stared at Jesse's nose. "What happened to you?"

"Lillard took a swing at me."

Keogh didn't comment further. He said, "I'm going after supper. Don't open the door for anyone but me and keep that shotgun close."

Jesse nodded. He held the door for Keogh and locked it after him. He was hungry, he discovered. He'd had nothing to eat since dawn.

Out back in the cell it was quiet. Jesse didn't want to look in on the prisoners but he knew he should. He crossed the office and opened the door. Keogh had lighted a lantern and hung it in the corridor. By its light, Jesse could see the two men sitting on a cot beneath the smashed window. They both looked at him but neither said anything. Jesse closed the door.

Jesse went to the broken window and stared out into the street. Glass still lay on the floor and crunched beneath his feet. More to keep busy than because it needed doing, he got a broom and dustpan and began to clean up the glass. When he had finished, he reached up and carefully pulled loose several sharp pieces that looked as if they might fall.

He heard a sudden shout from the prisoners' cell. He headed for the door leading to the cells, hearing the sound of breaking glass behind it as he did.

Before he reached it, a shot racketed, part of its sound coming through the closed door, part of it reaching him through the broken front window. He slammed open the door and plunged into the corridor, gun in hand.

The two prisoners had separated and now cowered in opposite corners of the cell. Jesse could smell powdersmoke but no one was visible in the window opening out of which the glass had been broken, just as it had earlier from the window opposite. He said, "Either of you hit?"

Both men answered shakily in the negative. Johnson said, "For God's sake, blow out that lantern. Next time he'll get one of us."

Jesse didn't believe it. Nobody in town wanted either of these two to get out of what they'd done so easily. The shot had been fired to scare them, to make more terrifying their stay in jail. But there was no use arguing. He blew out the lantern and returned to the office. He supposed he ought to look around the side of the jail to see if the man who had fired the shot was still there but since doing so would leave the jail temporarily unguarded, he stayed where he was.

His feeling of uneasiness was growing stronger all the time. He had never seen people as angry as they were in Pawnee Bluffs tonight. He had never seen anyone prepared to take the law into their own hands but tonight everybody in town seemed ready to. Furthermore, even if the townspeople did calm down, there was still Lillard and his crew. Lillard's men would do what he told them to. If he told them to take the prisoners out of jail and hang them, that was what would be done, and if the sheriff and deputy stood in the way, they'd only get themselves shot.

From outside, Keogh's voice called, "Open up, Jesse. It's me."

Jesse unbolted the door and held it so that Keogh could come in. Keogh carried in four stacked-up trays of food he had obtained at the hotel. Jesse bolted the door before taking two of them from him. He put them down on the desk, then crossed the office and opened the door leading to the cells. He went in first and relighted the lantern, over the scared protests of the prisoners. Keogh brought the trays and slid them under the barred cell door. Jesse said, "Somebody took a shot at them a while ago. They don't want the lantern lighted."

Keogh stared through the bars unsympathetically. "You'd just better hope somebody shoots you dead. It's the easiest way out of the fix you're in."

The men came across the cell and picked up their trays. They were like animals, Jesse thought, dirty, hairy, cowering like dogs that have been whipped. He hated them no less; he felt growing contempt for them.

He returned to the office. Keogh followed and closed the door. Jesse got one of the trays and sat down to eat. The rising racket in both saloons came through the broken window. His mouth full, Keogh said, "Workin' themselves up to what they're going to do."

"And what are *we* going to do?"

"See that they don't."

"Have you got any plan?"

Keogh shook his head.

"Do you think it'll come down to putting guns on them?"

"Likely will."

Jesse frowned. He thought it possible that Keogh did have some kind of plan, but the sheriff plainly wasn't ready to tell him what it was. He said, "You told me earlier you'd seen a lynching once. What was it like?"

Keogh chewed thoughtfully for a moment before he replied. Finally he said, "Just like this. Yelling. Shooting through the windows of the jail. Making threats."

"Were you sheriff then?"

"Nope. Deputy. About your age, I guess. It happened fast. One minute the town was about like this one is, and the next they had a telegraph pole using it for a battering ram on the door. The door went down and they came in. The sheriff fired a warning shot into the ceiling but it didn't even slow 'em down. They rolled over us and went back and took the prisoner out of his cell. He was down on his knees, begging and blubbering enough to make a man throw up, but they had something going in their veins that kept 'em from feeling anything, even disgust."

He paused for a moment, remembering. Finally he said, "A mob's a scary thing. It's like the men in it aren't even human anymore. You can't talk to them. You can't appeal to them. They've only got one thing in mind and that's to kill. Well, they hanged that poor devil and I don't know to this day whether he did what he was accused of or not. Nobody will ever know because he didn't get a trial."

"What about afterward?"

"Well, next morning he was still hanging there. A bunch of men came to the sheriff and told him to cut him down. He told them to go to hell. He hung there all day and I guess that made everything worse. Everybody started blaming everybody else. Those that hadn't been part of the mob were pretty blunt about blaming those that were. Among those that had been part of the mob, each blamed the others for getting them into it. Inside of a week, men who had been friends for years weren't speaking to each other anymore. The storekeepers started pressing people for their bills. By the time a month was up, a fourth of the people had just up and left. I went through that town five years afterward and there wasn't anything left of it. Just some empty buildings with their doors banging in the wind. No people. Everyone had gone."

Jesse asked, "What was the alternative? Suppose the sheriff had fired into them when they broke down the door? Would it have stopped them? Or would they just have killed the sheriff and you, too?"

Keogh shrugged. "I don't know. I've never seen that happen or talked to anybody that has. Maybe they'd have stopped. Maybe not."

"We may get a chance to find out."

Keogh studied him, plainly doubting that Jesse would kill to protect the lives of the pair out back. It was true that Jesse had pulled his gun on Fothergill and had made him believe that he would shoot. Later he had told Keogh that he would have fired. But that didn't mean he would.

Keogh said slowly, "I guess no man knows what he'll do at a time like that until it comes."

Jesse said, "Then maybe we'd better decide what we're going to do right now." He couldn't tell the sheriff what to do and he didn't even know what he'd do himself. If he had to weigh the lives of the decent people of the town against the scum out back. . . . He began to hope desperately that that decision would never have to be made.

CHAPTER 10

Sarah Lillard was almost immediately sorry that she had refused to see Jesse Marks. Sorry in a strangely contradictory kind of way. She still didn't want him to see her in her present condition, with her hair a mess, her face bruised and swollen almost to the point where she was unrecognizable. When she faced Jesse she at least wanted to look decently presentable. It was enough to have between them those other things that had happened to her without feeling that she looked terrible besides.

How was Jesse going to feel about what had been done to her? It would be comforting to assure herself that it would make no difference to him, that he would understand that it had been in no way her fault. Still, she knew every man wanted to be the first.

And even if Jesse could overlook what had happened, could *she* forget it after they were married? Her treatment at the hands of the two men had been brutal and ugly. Mercifully she had been unconscious part of the time. But not all of it. Wouldn't she inevitably compare her relationship with Jesse with her treatment at the hands of those other two? And how could she be the kind of wife Jesse deserved if she was making such comparisons in her mind?

Her feeling of depression increased and suddenly she wished that she could just die. Jesse had come to see her but he probably had not really wanted to see her at all. He had only come for appearance' sake, and probably had been relieved when she'd refused to talk to him. Eventually she would get well, and would get up out of this bed, and everybody in Pawnee Bluffs would try to pretend that everything was just the way it used to be. But she would know and so would they that everything was not the same. They'd whisper behind her back. "That's Sarah Lillard. She was raped and thrown off a cliff by those two men that got hanged. Jesse Marks was going to marry her but he changed his mind after what happened to her."

The door opened and her mother came into the room. Sarah suddenly realized that Melissa had not been in to see her and wondered why. She asked, "Where's Melissa? Why hasn't she come?"

The question brought a strange expression to her mother's face. Mrs. Lillard looked away quickly and walked to the window, turning her back to Sarah. Sarah said, "Mother?"

"What?" Her mother didn't turn.

"Where's Melissa? Why hasn't she been in?"

Her mother did not immediately reply. When she did, she said unconvincingly, "We thought you were too badly hurt. We thought that she should wait."

Sarah felt something cold, like a ball, growing in her chest. She said, "Mother, look at me."

"Why?" Her mother didn't turn.

"Because I want to see your face. Something's happened to Melissa, hasn't it?"

"What makes you say that?" Mrs. Lillard turned. Her jaw was firm and so was her mouth but there was a shine of tears in her eyes.

Suddenly Sarah knew. Something had happened to Melissa, too. Those men . . . She said shrilly, "Mother, I want to know! Where is Melissa? Is she hurt, too?"

The tears welled out of Mrs. Lillard's eyes and ran across her cheeks. Her face contorted and a tortured sob broke from her lips. She crossed the room and fell to her knees beside Sarah's bed. She buried her face. The words came from her as if they had been torn out by force. "Melissa's gone."

"What do you mean *gone?* I thought . . ."

Mrs. Lillard brought her weeping under control long enough to cry, "She's dead! Melissa's dead. They threw her over the cliff, too, but . . ."

For a long time Sarah was numb. Her mind simply would not accept the fact that Melissa was dead. She asked, "How? She wasn't anywhere near. How could they . . . ?"

"She . . . followed you." Mrs. Lillard began to weep anew.

"Did they . . . did they do the same thing to Melissa that they did to me?"

Mrs. Lillard shook her head without raising it. "I don't think so."

"But you don't know?"

Again Mrs. Lillard shook her head. Sarah turned her face toward the door. She screamed for Doctor Peabody and he came almost immediately, his face somber with concern.

Sarah didn't know the words to describe what had been done to her but she had to know if the same thing had happened to Melissa, despite her age. She cried excitedly, "What about Melissa, Doctor? Did they do the same things to her that they did to me?"

Peabody shook his head. "No, Sarah."

"You're sure?"

"Yes, Sarah. I'm sure. They threw her off the cliff but they didn't hurt her beforehand."

Sarah felt her own tears coming like a scalding flood. Her face contorted the way her mother's had. She buried her face in the pillow, holding it with both hands. But even muffled by the pillow, the tortured sounds of her sobs came out.

Peabody lifted Mrs. Lillard bodily. He guided her toward the door firmly despite Mrs. Lillard's apparent wish to stay.

He pushed her out and followed her, closing the door behind.

The dam of grief had finally broken in Sarah Lillard's mind. She was wracked with it and torn with wild sobbing. But Peabody knew that weeping would be good for her. He had been hoping she would break down. Having released all her pent-up terror, she could begin to heal.

Mrs. Lillard stood in the darkness of the Peabody porch, dabbing at her tears with a soggy handkerchief. She ached for Sarah. She ached herself when she thought of Melissa lying dead. She could hear loud voices in the darkness down the street a way and recognized one of them as her husband's, the other as that of Galen Sauls. They came closer and finally she saw their two shadowy figures. Sauls opened the gate and both men came up the gravel path.

Lillard said harshly, "Don't let that sonofabitch in again! Do you understand?"

Mrs. Lillard could feel her anger rising. What right had he to be so cruel and callous at a time like this? Couldn't he wait at least until Sarah was well enough to get out of bed?

With more show of spirit than she had displayed in all her years of marriage to him, she said, "Jesse Marks will see Sarah anytime he wishes to. She needs him now and I won't keep him away from her." Her voice was firm and strong, showing none of the terror she felt inside.

For a moment Lillard stared at her unbelievingly. Then her defiance fed the growing anger inside of him. Unthinkingly, he swung his hand and the flat of it struck her cheek with a sound that could have been heard fifty feet away. Her head rocked to one side and she staggered away from the door, fighting to keep her feet.

Lillard didn't even look at her. He slammed open the door and stomped into Doc Peabody's parlor, Galen Sauls at his heels, clutching at him and trying to hold him back.

Both Doc and Mrs. Peabody had heard the argument outside. They stood in the middle of the room, staring at him. Without speaking, he crossed the room and went into the room where Sarah was.

Her weeping had stopped because she, too, had heard the disturbance on the porch. She had never heard her parents fight before. She had never known her mother to speak up against her father. White-faced, her cheeks wet with tears, she stared at her father.

For an instant he didn't speak, as if, for once, he was feeling compassion for her. Then his face reddened as he let his anger take control. He shouted, "Damn it, I told you not to see him again!"

Color began to return to her face but for the moment she was too surprised to speak. Lillard saw the growing defiance in her expression, though, and roared, "This wouldn't have happened if you'd done what you ought! Now, by God, I'm telling you. I'm not asking anymore. Don't see Jesse Marks again!"

Sarah was so furious that she was trembling. There was absolutely no color in her face. She said evenly, "Why? Are you afraid I might catch a bullet meant for him? The way Mrs. Keogh did?"

He surged across the room and stood above her, hand raised to strike. Sauls rushed after him and caught his arm. For an instant Lillard resisted him, and there was a brief tussle. Sauls pleaded, "Boss! You'll be sorry!"

It might have been better all around if Sarah could have held her tongue. But she was thoroughly infuriated now. She said, "I'll tell you one thing. A bullet would be better than what my mother got, married all these years to you."

Sauls gave her a despairing glance. Lillard yanked away his arm. He crossed to the bed and this time he did strike her, on the side of the face.

The side he struck was already bruised and the blow hurt much more than it ordinarily would have. Tears welled up in her eyes from the pain, but it was not the tears that shocked Lillard into immobility. It was the look in Sarah's eyes. Never in his life had he seen such hatred, such contempt.

He might have apologized, but he got no chance. Sarah's mother came storming into the room and bodily shoved him aside. She positioned herself between Sarah's bed and Lillard. Never before today had she stood up to him. But doing so a few moments before on the porch seemed to have given her courage she had never been able to muster before. She said, "I am leaving you, Reuben. I will take a room at the hotel and will send for my things. When she is well enough, Sarah will come with me."

She looked as if she expected a lightning bolt to strike her dead. When it did not, her back straightened a little and she raised her head. Lillard stared at her as if he had never seen her before. He didn't seem to know what to say or what to do. Finally, mumbling something indistinguishable, he turned and stalked from the room. He went through the outside door and would have slammed it except that Sauls was immediately behind. He stormed down the gravel walk, slammed open the gate so violently that he broke one of its boards, and mounted his horse.

Sauls was twenty-five feet behind. Lillard mounted, whirled the horse with a savage yank on the reins, and dug spurs viciously into the horse's sides. The horse jumped forward and broke into an instant run.

Sauls stood at the gate, staring after him. He knew there was no use trying to catch up. He knew Lillard needed time to cool off before he would even listen to reason, if he ever would.

Sauls mounted and headed for the center of town. Tonight, Lillard was an extremely dangerous man. He had lost Melissa when she was killed. Now he had lost both Sarah and his wife.

He would never blame himself. Instead, he would blame the two men being held in jail. He would take his vengeance against them.

CHAPTER 11

Jesse was on his way to the hotel with the empty supper trays when he saw Reuben Lillard come thundering down the street. His horse was at full gallop and as he rounded the corner he nearly collided with a man on foot. The man jumped, slipped, and fell, then got up quickly, barely in time to avoid Galen Sauls's horse, thundering around the corner in pursuit.

Jesse stopped and stared. Lillard hauled his horse to a plunging halt in front of the Pawnee Saloon, with Sauls close behind. Lillard went inside while Sauls led the frightened horses to the tie rail.

Jesse continued toward the front door of the hotel. Passing Sauls in front of the saloon, he nodded brusquely. Sauls grinned faintly and whistled with awe, apparently at Lillard's towering rage. Thus encouraged, Jesse asked, "Another fight?"

Sauls nodded. He plainly wanted to talk to Jesse but it was as plain that he felt doing so would be disloyal. Jesse asked, "Is Sarah all right?"

Sauls nodded. He went into the saloon and Jesse went on into the hotel with his trays. He left them on the desk, went out again, and walked back toward the jail.

There was no boisterousness in the saloon, but there was loud talk, all of it intemperate. Jesse stopped for a moment to see if he could hear anything. He heard the words "hang the sonsabitches" and "They didn't give those girls no trial, did they?"

He went on. He hoped the sheriff had a plan, and he hoped

the plan included getting the killers out of town. If they remained here, they'd decorate a scaffold before the night was through.

The jail door was locked. He knocked and when Keogh asked who it was he said, "Jesse," and Keogh let him in.

Keogh, also, had apparently seen Lillard riding down the street because he asked, "What's eating Lillard now?"

"Another fight is what Sauls said. I suppose with Sarah, or his wife, or both. I've seen him mad but never as mad as that."

Keogh studied him. Jesse grinned. "You can stop worrying about me. I don't want a lynching any more than you do. But I do know that if you keep those two here, in town, they're not going to make it through the night."

"I wasn't planning to keep them here."

"How are you going to get them out? And where are you taking them?"

"Colorado City."

"That's seventy-five miles away."

"Yep." Keogh studied Jesse carefully. "You'd better think. If you help me get them away, any chance you've got of making it up with Lillard will be gone. Sarah may even hate you for it because it will mean she'll have to go all the way to Colorado City to testify. Before strangers."

Jesse said, "I've thought. I'll help."

"All right. Leo Espinosa is about the same build as that skinny one. Nels Hansen is about the same size as Johnson. Both of them are good, solid men that we can trust. You go get them and tell them to come to the jail."

Jesse nodded. He went out, closing the door behind him. He heard the bolt shoot home as the sheriff locked it behind him. A locked door was only an uncertain barrier at best because of the window that had been broken earlier.

The streets were almost deserted since most of the townsmen were in one or the other of the two saloons. Jesse hurried along the street. Espinosa lived in a small, adobe house down near the creek. Hansen lived uptown several doors from Doc Peabody. Jesse hoped both men would be at home and that he wouldn't have to go into the saloons after them. He thought that of all the men in town, Espinosa and Hansen were the two least likely to be shouting for lynching the prisoners. Both men had served as sheriff's deputies.

There was a lamp burning in Espinosa's house. Jesse went into the small patio and knocked. Mrs. Espinosa answered the door. Immediately she said, "Jesse Marks! Come in! Leo thought the sheriff might be wanting him before very long."

Jesse went inside. Three small children peered at him shyly from a doorway. Espinosa was a short, thin man, dark-skinned. His usually smiling face was serious. "Trouble?"

"Not yet, but it looks like there's going to be. The sheriff wants you down at the jail."

Espinosa nodded and headed into the next room to get his gun. Jesse waited. Espinosa returned carrying a double-barreled shotgun that looked like a ten-gauge. He kissed his wife and followed Jesse out the door. Jesse left him immediately, saying, "I'm going after Nels."

He hurried up the narrow back street, not wanting to see anyone, not wanting to be seen. He didn't want anybody carrying the word that he was moving through town rounding up help. The less that was known, the better chance the sheriff's plan had of working.

Hansen's house was on the same street as Peabody's, and four doors away. There was no activity in front of Peabody's but Sarah's window showed a light. There were lights in Hansen's house, too. Jesse twisted the bell. Downtown it hadn't looked as if anybody had stayed at home, but obviously a few of the townspeople had.

Mrs. Hansen, big and rawboned, answered the door and

her pleasant, Scandinavian face wreathed itself with smiles. "Come in, Jesse. Do you want Nels?"

"Yes, ma'am. The sheriff does." He could smell cabbage that had been cooked for supper. Nels came from the kitchen, a big man getting heavy in middle age. A man that could wear Johnson's clothes, thought Jesse, and look like him.

The sheriff hadn't outlined the plan, but Jesse thought he could guess what it was. Keogh would have Hansen and Espinosa change clothes with the prisoners. Then he would take them out, as if trying to spirit them away from town. He would make sure that he was seen. Then, after the mob of infuriated townsmen had followed him, planning to take the prisoners away from him, Jesse would slip away with the two killers and take them to Colorado City. It was a desperate plan and a risky one because Jesse would be alone. But it was better than no plan at all.

Jesse said, "Sheriff Keogh wants you, Nels. I'll go down with you." He doubted if it mattered whether Espinosa and Hansen were seen going into the jail. Everybody knew they had served as sheriff's deputies and would assume they were doing so again.

Hansen went out and Jesse followed him. If Mrs. Hansen was concerned it didn't show. The door closed.

Even from here they could hear the noise downtown. It was just a low rumble or murmur in the air. Hansen said, "Sounds like they're getting all worked up."

"Uh-huh. They're making lynch talk already but the sheriff figures they'll have to be a lot drunker before they actually get around to it."

"What's he going to do?"

"He didn't say, but I figure he's going to try getting them away."

After that, they walked hurriedly side by side. Jesse detoured at the corner of the block that held the hotel, saloon, and jail, and went back to the alley. They reached the jail and came around on the far side of it. Jesse knocked and Keogh opened the door. Nels went in. Jesse said, "I'll get some horses and bring them around in back."

Keogh nodded. He said, "After you do that, get three for yourself, without being seen. Tie them someplace where there's no chance of anybody finding them."

"All right." The door closed and Jesse crossed the street to the livery barn. The horses they'd ridden in on earlier and those ridden by the two prisoners had been taken to the livery barn, probably by John Lucas, the liveryman. Or else they'd gone there on their own.

The place was dark and the tackroom where Lucas usually could be found was dark. Jesse walked along the long aisle between the stalls. He went to the rear doors, which stood open when the weather was good. There was a corral out back containing eight or ten horses.

Jesse took three halters from pegs on the stable wall and went into the corral. He caught three horses at random and led them out. He led them into the stable. Up front, he got saddle blankets, saddles, and bridles. When all three horses were saddled, he led them out the front doors and down the wooden ramp to the street. He knew it was practically a certainty that he and the horses would be seen. They'd be duly reported to the men in the saloon, who would know immediately what they were for. Lookouts would be posted so that the men would know when the sheriff and his prisoners left town.

He led the horses across, hurrying as though he did not want to be seen. A glance up the street told him he had been seen by two men in front of the Pawnee Saloon. They immediately turned and went inside.

Jesse continued to the rear of the jail, where he tied the three horses. Having done so, he hurried along the alley toward the lower end of town. As soon as he figured he had gone far enough, he cut through weed-grown vacant lots back to Bluff Street and, crossing it, went on to the alley behind the livery barn. This time he entered the livery barn through the rear doors. He got three saddles, three bridles, and three saddle blankets out of the tackroom and carried them to the corral gate out back. He was more careful in his selection of horses this time, picking animals that looked like they could travel tirelessly. He saddled and bridled them. Mounting one, he led the other two down the alley toward the creek. Reaching it, he tied all three in a thick grove of trees and walked back toward the jail.

Everything was ready, and he knew there was a good chance the plan would work. But its ultimate success depended on how far away from town the sheriff, Espinosa, and Hansen got before they were overtaken by the mob.

Jesse reached the jail by way of the alley at the rear and slipped silently to the front. He didn't see anyone this time, but he had the feeling he was being watched from the moment he left the alley shadows. He knocked lightly and the sheriff let him in.

Espinosa and Hansen had not yet changed clothes with the prisoners, probably because of the chance that someone might come to the jail. They sat talking to the sheriff, their faces sober and maybe even a little scared. Keogh asked, "Everything ready?"

Jesse nodded. "There's three horses tied out back. I know I was seen leading them across the street and I figure somebody's watching the jail so they'll spot you when you leave."

"What about the others?"

"They're tied down in the bed of the creek."

"Think you were seen?"

Jesse shook his head. "I'm almost sure I wasn't. I crossed

the street two blocks down and I came into the stable from the rear."

Keogh nodded approvingly. Jesse asked, "How soon are you going to go?"

"Pretty soon." Keogh looked at the clock. It was not quite seven-thirty. He said, "Eight or thereabouts, I suppose."

"Maybe you ought to give them time to get a little more whiskey inside of them."

"They'll have enough, judging from the noise."

Jesse said, "I don't envy you when they catch up and find how they've been fooled."

"They'll be mad, but they won't do anything."

"I hope you're right." Jesse suspected that his own job was the more hazardous of the two, even if he didn't have anybody after him. The two prisoners would do their best to kill him and escape, knowing it was the last chance they'd get. And if they got away, Jesse wouldn't dare go back to Pawnee Bluffs.

Not only that, but if he killed the prisoners trying to escape, Keogh would never believe it had been unavoidable.

And even if he did get the prisoners safely to Colorado City, he'd be universally disliked for it in Pawnee Bluffs. Sarah would probably hate him and her father would hate him even more bitterly than he did now.

He shrugged. He was committed and the less thinking he did about the consequences the better off he was going to be.

CHAPTER 12

The knock on the jail door was so timid and soft that none of the four men heard it at first. When they did, Keogh nodded toward the door leading to the cells, indicating that Espinosa and Hansen were to conceal themselves. When they had, he opened the door. Jesse stood back, the shotgun in his hands.

He lowered it immediately when he saw who was at the door. It was Mrs. Lillard, white-faced and scared, looking ten years older than when Jesse had seen her last. Her eyes were red from weeping.

She said in a scared voice, "Good evening, Sheriff."

"Come in, Mrs. Lillard." Keogh stood aside and Mrs. Lillard came timidly into the room. Keogh closed and locked the door.

She looked at Jesse. "Sarah wants to see you, Jesse. She asked me to come for you."

Jesse glanced at Keogh, who agreed by nodding his head. Jesse opened the door, handing the shotgun to Keogh as he went out. He closed the door behind them. Mrs. Lillard said, "I came down the alley. Do you mind if we go back the same way?"

"No." He took her arm and they walked through the weeds at the side of the jail. She did not comment on the three horses tied behind the jail.

Jesse wanted to tell her he was sorry about Lillard's temper outburst but he didn't do so. She had herself under control but he suspected that it wouldn't take much to make her lose it and start weeping again.

He was surprised that Sarah had asked to see him after so steadfastly refusing to do so earlier. Her father's outburst must have brought on the change of heart.

They reached Doc Peabody's house by way of the alley behind it, and cut through the yard to the front. Mrs. Lillard knocked lightly and the door opened. Mrs. Peabody let them in and quietly closed the door.

Peabody had been standing at the window looking out. His face was worried as he turned. "Still quiet?"

Jesse said, "So far."

"Sarah wants to see you."

Jesse nodded. Peabody said, "I told you this before but I'm going to caution you again. Her face is badly bruised and swollen. You'll be shocked when you see her but it's extremely important that you don't let her know you're shocked. Sarah needs reassurance right now more than anything. She's just had a terrible row with her father."

Jesse said, "Yes, sir."

"All right then, go on in." Peabody still seemed a little doubtful about the wisdom of Jesse doing so.

Jesse was scared as he approached the door to Sarah's room. Could he look at her bruised, swollen, battered face and not let his own face show some kind of dismay? He grabbed the knob and forced himself to open the door.

There was a single lamp burning on the dresser. Sarah's hair was loose, freshly brushed, spread out on the pillow on both sides of her head. Jesse needn't have worried. He was shocked all right when he saw her face, but it wasn't the shock that showed. It was the outraged anger of a man very much in love.

For an instant he stood there in the middle of the room, looking at her while her eyes fearfully searched his face. Then tears welled up and wild sobs wracked her body. Jesse crossed the room and dropped to his knees beside the bed. Gently, ever so gently, he laid his cheek against hers so that he wouldn't hurt her more.

Her arms went around his neck with strength that surprised him and then he was holding her in his arms. The wild, hysterical sobbing grew worse, bringing a veritable flood of tears.

How long it continued this way, Jesse couldn't have said. Conflicting emotions tore through him—fury that anyone could have hurt this girl so terribly, pity for her pain and grief, love, tenderness. . . . He heard the door open behind him and turned his head. Peabody stood in the doorway and Jesse stared questioningly at him, mutely asking him what he ought to do.

Peabody only smiled. He closed the door, and Jesse guessed he must have done all right. Now, perhaps, Sarah would begin to heal, both outside and in.

Her sobbing gradually diminished and finally stopped. Jesse drew away, smiled at her and gently wiped the tears from her cheeks with the palm of his hand. Again her eyes searched his, looking for some sign from him that what had happened had changed the way things were between them. She didn't find it because it wasn't there and finally a small smile touched the corners of her mouth. She pulled his head to her and kissed him on the nose.

Jesse cleared his throat so that his voice would come out as steadily as he wished it to. He said, "You get well fast. No matter what your father says, we're going to be married as soon as you're able to get up."

Her smile widened and she nodded wordlessly. Jesse kissed her again and got to his feet. "I've got to go back. But I'll come again tomorrow." He knew that wasn't true, but he didn't want to spoil this moment by telling her what he had to do. Peabody could explain it to her tomorrow.

He went to the door. He looked back at her as he opened it, realizing that his own eyes were damp. He brushed at them impatiently before he stepped out into the room where the others were.

Mrs. Lillard smiled at him approvingly. He said, "Doctor, will you come outside for a minute?"

Peabody followed him out. Jesse told him about the plan for getting the prisoners out of town. "I told her I'd be in to see her tomorrow but I won't be able to. Will you explain to her?"

"Of course I will." Jesse started away and Peabody called after him, "Be careful, Jesse. That girl can't stand any more bad shocks."

"Yes, sir." Jesse hurried through the yard to the alley and headed for the jail.

Reuben Lillard strode furiously into the saloon, with Galen Sauls following as soon as he had finished tying the horses to the rail. The bar was crowded. Lillard shouldered through roughly, pushing men aside, hoping wickedly that somebody would object. Nobody did. One look at Lillard's face was enough to give them second thoughts.

Halverson was behind the bar tonight, and so was Henry Ortiz, who tended bar when Halverson was off. Both men were busy and sweating in the overheated, smoky atmosphere of the place. Ortiz came hurrying and Lillard said harshly, "Whiskey. Two glasses." Ortiz brought the bottle and glasses and Lillard half filled both of them. Sauls came up beside him. The men on that side made room for Sauls. Sauls started to say something, then changed his mind after looking at Lillard's face. He picked up the glass Lillard had provided for him and gulped down the liquor. He wiped his mouth with the back of his hand.

Lillard felt mean and wanted to hit somebody, but he knew better than to start a row with anybody in this room, however much he might feel like it, because he was liable to need all of these men. Besides, there was no reason for him to pick a quarrel with anybody here. His quarrel was with his wife. He poured himself a second drink and gulped that, too.

Damn her! Damn her! Where the hell did she get off, talking to him the way she had? And where the hell did Sarah get off, defying him?

He gulped another drink, knowing he shouldn't down them so fast but not really giving a damn. So what if he did get drunk? Nobody had a better right. His youngest daughter had been brutally murdered, thrown off the cliff to her death as if she had been so much trash. Sarah had been raped by the two men sitting safely and smugly over there in the jail right now.

He wasn't going to stand for it. He wasn't going to go home tonight, and sleep, as if nothing had happened to rip apart his family and his life. He wasn't going to let those two go to trial because if they did it would mean that Sarah would be put on the witness stand, required to identify them and tell in detail what they had done to her. She had been, by her own admission, unconscious when they threw her off the cliff, so she wouldn't be able to say that they were the ones who had thrown her off. It therefore would boil down to trying them for rape, and she would have to go into all the details up in front of a big courtroom crowd. Doing that would ruin her for life. What man would want a wife who had been abused that way?

Sauls stood beside him, staring moodily at his empty glass. Lillard said, "Have another."

Obediently, Sauls poured himself another drink. There was

a faint note of hopefulness in his voice as he asked, "You going home tonight or staying in town?"

Lillard glared at him. He said harshly, "I ain't going home again until those two dirty bastards are dead."

Sauls didn't reply. Instead he picked up his glass. Lillard said, "I want those two men dead before the sun comes up! I want them hanging side by side from that old cottonwood!"

His voice was heard by men on both sides, and suddenly they quieted. They stared at Lillard expectantly. He could see, by looking into their faces, that they didn't like him. They probably never had. He was the wealthiest man in the county and that in itself was enough to make him disliked. Furthermore, he suspected that his personality wasn't the kind that won a man a lot of friends. But tonight every man in this room had placed himself in Lillard's shoes. They were imagining how they, themselves, would feel if it had been their wives or their daughters who had been thrown off the cliff west of town. They would help him with whatever he wanted done.

Halverson looked across the bar at him. He said, "Every man here is behind you, Mr. Lillard. There's more that feel the same way down at the Pink Lady. You just tell us what to do."

Loud enough to be heard throughout the suddenly quiet saloon, Lillard said, "I don't want them to go to trial because of what it'll do to Sarah when she's forced to testify."

There was a rumble of agreement from the men. Lillard went on, "We know they did it. The sheriff and his deputy trailed them from the place it happened. There just ain't any doubt."

Again the rumble. Lillard said, "Neither the sheriff nor his deputy will do anything if we all go over there after them. They'll point guns at us and they'll threaten to shoot, but when the chips are down, they won't. We can go in and get the prisoners and have it over with."

Suddenly the crowd was quiet. A man nervously cleared his throat in the back of the room. Somebody yelled, "What if you're wrong? What if the sheriff does shoot?"

Lillard yelled, "I'll be right in the front! If he shoots, I'll take the charge!"

Jed Brown, one of Lillard's crewmen, came into the saloon. He crossed to Lillard and Sauls. He said, "Boss, it looks like the sheriff is going to try and get the prisoners away. Jesse Marks just got three horses from the livery stable and tied them behind the jail."

Everybody in the saloon suddenly began to talk at once. Lillard raised his hands. When the room had quieted he said, "Maybe this is better. We'll wait until they go and then catch 'em out away from town. All of you that want to help, slip out one at a time and get your horses and guns. Tie 'em out behind the saloon. Go out two or three at a time, and that way maybe the sheriff won't know we're on to him."

Several men near the door went out. Lillard waited for a few minutes and then nodded at three more, who left immediately. Lillard said, "Sauls, you and Brown go out and keep a watch on the jail. When you see them leave, follow them. As soon as you figure out where they're headed, one of you come back and let us know."

Sauls and Brown went out the door. The saloon was less noisy now and nobody was yelling anymore. Before this development, it had all been talk. Now they faced the prospect of taking action. It excited some but it scared others. Lillard knew that less than half of these men would actually go along with him.

He spoke to a man immediately beside him. "Mind going down to the Pink Lady and telling them what's going on?"

The man shook his head and hurried out. Lillard poured himself another drink but he didn't gulp this one. He sipped it slowly. He couldn't afford to be fuzzy-headed when they all rode out of here.

He ought to be excited and pleased that everybody was backing him, that before the sun came up the prisoners were going to be dead. But he wasn't excited and he wasn't pleased. He was facing the prospect, instead, of going home tomorrow to an empty house, to a house that would remain empty because neither Sarah nor his wife would ever be coming home to it again.

He knew, suddenly, that he had been a fool, mooning over a dead woman all these years. He had neglected Mary. He had taken her for granted and now it was too late.

Angrily he put thoughts of Sarah and Mary from his mind. Tonight he only had one thing to do. That was to see to it that the men over in the jail died hanging by a rope.

CHAPTER 13

At eight o'clock Keogh said, "All right. Let's go out back and get ready." He opened the door leading to the cells. Espinosa and Nels Hansen went through and Keogh and Jesse followed them. Keogh handed the shotgun to Jesse. He unlocked the cell door and said, "You two take off your clothes and throw them out here."

"What for?" Johnson asked.

"We're going to try getting you out of town. These two men are going to wear your clothes and I'm going to leave with them. If we're lucky, all the townsmen that are howling for your blood will follow us. When they do, my deputy will take you two and head for Colorado City."

"What if you're not lucky?"

"Then you'll get hanged. But if we don't do something, you're going to get hanged anyway. Now move. Take off your clothes and throw them out."

The two men began taking off their clothes. Underneath, their long underwear was filthy. Keogh picked up the outer clothes distastefully. He handed it to Hansen and Espinosa. "I hate to ask you to wear this stuff, but there's no other way."

Both Espinosa and Hansen showed their own distaste as they took off their clothes and put on the clothing of the prisoners. It smelled. Even Jesse could smell it from where he stood, holding the shotgun by the door. Keogh tossed the clothes Espinosa and Hansen had taken off to the prisoners.

They put it on, then sat down on the cot and pulled on their boots.

Standing there holding the shotgun, Jesse couldn't help thinking how easily he could solve this dirty problem that faced him, the sheriff, and the town. All he had to do was pull the trigger on the shotgun. One load of buckshot from the ten-gauge would kill both prisoners. His own problem would be solved. So would Keogh's. So would Sarah's, and so would the town's.

And why shouldn't he? There wasn't any doubt about the prisoners' guilt. One way or another, they were going to pay for their crimes with their lives. Why not now, before any of the townsmen got hurt or killed? Why not now, before they were lynched or before the sheriff or his deputies got killed defending them?

He shifted the muzzle of the shotgun until it covered the pair in the cell. The bars would deflect some of the buckshot, but not enough to keep most of the charge from striking the prisoners.

Johnson glanced up as he started to rise from the edge of the cot. He looked into the gaping muzzle of the double barrels. He raised his glance and stared at Jesse's face. He saw what was in Jesse's eyes and froze, afraid to do anything that would precipitate sudden action on Jesse's part. He held Jesse's glance and in his eyes was the same expression Jesse had once seen in the eyes of a rabid dog he had been forced to shoot.

Jesse felt Keogh watching him, and glanced at the sheriff. Keogh was just looking at him. Like Johnson, Keogh was afraid to either speak or move for fear doing so would make Jesse shoot. Jesse said, "It's a way out. They're going to die anyway and this way nobody else will get hurt."

"Except you. Hansen and Espinosa are witnesses. I'd have to bring you to trial."

"There isn't a jury in five hundred miles that would convict me."

Keogh shrugged. "Then go ahead and shoot."

Jesse held his rigid position for a minute more. Then, slowly and reluctantly, he lowered the gun and eased down the hammer.

Keogh didn't say anything. He closed and locked the cell door and handed Jesse the key. Hansen and Espinosa, a little white-faced from the scare they'd just had, followed him into the office. Jesse closed the door. Keogh turned out the lamp. He went to the front door and opened it. He peered into the street.

He stood there for a long time, letting his eyes become accustomed to the dark, studying the shadows across the street. Finally he beckoned to Hansen and Espinosa. He herded them out before him, his rifle out in front of him, leveled at their backs. Jesse remained in the doorway, shotgun ready, also studying the shadows across the street. He saw one man move slightly in a passageway between two buildings. He didn't see anything else, but that didn't mean there was nothing there. Keogh, Espinosa, and Hansen disappeared around the corner of the building.

Nothing moved in the street for almost a minute. Then, halfway to the corner, two horsemen came through a vacant lot and crossed the street. Jesse continued to watch. Five minutes passed. Ten, then, at last, he heard the hoofbeats of a single horse. A rider came up the street. He stared toward the jail as he passed but Jesse, in complete darkness, doubted if he had been seen. The man pulled up in front of the Pawnee Saloon and got down from his horse. He went inside.

Almost immediately there was a general exodus from the saloon. Jesse pulled back and closed the door. He went to the broken window and stood there, looking out.

Downstreet, men were pouring from the Pink Lady Saloon, too. They must have readied their horses earlier and tied them in alleys and vacant lots because less than five minutes later the street was filled with riders.

Jesse drew back farther into the room. There were a few muffled shouts and then the column of horsemen rode down the street at a walk. Jesse counted twenty-eight horsemen in all.

The plan was working. Lillard, if he was the one who had taken charge, had posted two lookouts across the street. They probably had already known about the three horses Jesse had saddled and tied out back. The two lookouts had followed Keogh when he left with Hansen and Espinosa. One had come back to report as soon as they had ascertained in which direction Keogh was heading.

Jesse knew that the sheriff would try to stay ahead of the mob for as long as possible. He'd try to give Jesse and the prisoners several hours' start. But that might not be possible. It was important that Jesse get started as soon as he could.

He got a handful of shells for the ten-gauge out of the drawer. He checked to make sure his revolver was in place at his side. He got two pairs of handcuffs out of another drawer, along with a key, which he dropped into his pocket. Carrying the cell key, he headed for the prisoners' cell.

He said, "All right, it looks clear now. They've all followed the sheriff and maybe we can get away." He inserted the key into the lock.

Before opening the door, he leaned the shotgun against the cell door across the passageway. Cuffs in hand, he swung back the door and stepped into the darkened cell.

Jesse Marks was not a fool. He did not step into the cell as unwarily as a sheep into a cage of wolves. He expected to be attacked and he was ready for it, even hoping for it. Conscience, duty, obligation, and decency had kept him from shooting the two prisoners a few minutes before. Nothing in his character or position denied him this.

One of the prisoners was waiting in the darkness on his left. The other was on his right. Their eyes were accustomed to the darkness, but Jesse's were, too. He felt them, glimpsed their movement as they rushed him simultaneously from both sides.

Tense with savage anticipation, Jesse yanked the door closed behind him. Before they reached him, he leaped forward and heard them come together even as he whirled. The two pairs of handcuffs in his hand weren't lethal weapons, but they were heavy enough to hurt if not to render unconsciousness. He swung them and felt them strike and heard Johnson, the larger of the two, cry out with pain.

Before Johnson could seize the loose-swinging handcuffs, Jesse pulled them back. At the same time he kicked out at Schwartz, coming at him with a club made from a leg wrenched from the cot. Jesse caught the club on the shoulder and pain shot through it, but he felt his foot connect with Schwartz and knew from the man's sudden indrawing of breath and subsequent groan that he had caught him in the crotch. Schwartz bent double and Jesse brought up his knee with as much force as he could muster, catching Schwartz squarely in the face. The man collapsed to the floor, spitting and wheezing and groaning from the pain of the kick.

That left Johnson, who suddenly had halted his rush and now stood in a half crouch, waiting for Jesse to come to him. Jesse obliged. It was not quite pitch black in the cell. A little light from stars and from the front of the hotel came in the barred window high up on the wall. Jesse could see Johnson, not his face nor individual features, but his form. He could see well enough to fight.

He was thinking that it was Johnson who had to have initiated the attack on Sarah. Johnson had begun it and Schwartz had gone along with it. Fierce and eager in the darkness, he suddenly lunged forward, swinging the handcuffs like a whip.

Again they slashed across Johnson's face, cutting, hurting, bringing another outcry of pain. This time Johnson's grab for them was successful. His hand clutched them and held on.

Jesse lay back against the pull on the handcuffs, yanking Johnson toward him. Johnson came stumbling across the cell, releasing the handcuffs too late to keep himself from being pulled completely off balance.

Jesse dropped the handcuffs and as Johnson went by, seized him by the collar with both hands. Using Johnson's own momentum and adding all he could to it, he ran with the man, carrying him the rest of the way across the cell and slamming him headlong into the stone outside wall. The sound was solid as his head struck it and he collapsed at the foot of the wall.

Jesse turned his head. Schwartz was up, coming at him again with the club. This time Jesse did not use his foot. He waited, avoiding Schwartz's swing with the club by stepping back, and then bored in. He caught Schwartz squarely in the nose with a hard right fist exactly where his knee had caught it less than a minute before. All the fight went instantly out of Schwartz. He collapsed to his knees, his hands went to his face, and he began to whimper like a hurt dog.

Breathing hard, Jesse picked up the handcuffs. He yanked Schwartz's hands behind his back and cuffed them tightly. Crossing the cell, he cuffed Johnson, who was unconscious, similarly. He went back to the cell door, picked up the shotgun, and returned to the office. There was a bucket half full of water on the washstand. He carried it back and threw it into Johnson's face.

The man came to, sputtering. Jesse waited. There had been no pleasure in beating the two men. It hadn't been the way he'd thought it would. He could only feel disgust, both with himself and with the two sorry creatures now groveling on the floor of the cell.

Harshly he said, "Get on your feet. Keep your damn mouths shut unless you want the townspeople who are still in town to string you up."

Schwartz staggered out of the cell. Johnson stumbled after him. They went into the front office and stood, cowed and silent, beside the door.

Jesse picked up the shotgun. He broke it and by feel checked both its loads. He crossed the room and peered out the broken window into the street.

There wasn't a person in sight. He could see the light squares cast on the walk and into the street by the windows of the Pawnee Saloon and the Pawnee Hotel, next to it. Farther downstreet, light was thrown into the street from the windows of the Pink Lady Saloon. He said, "Stand aside."

They obeyed silently. Jesse knew they weren't likely to put up any more resistance, at least as long as they remained in town. They didn't know where the horses were and they had overwhelming respect for the fury of the townspeople after the experience they'd had getting to the jail.

Jesse opened the door. He peered out again, taking a full minute to study the shadows across the street. He saw nothing, heard nothing but the faint barking of a dog several blocks away.

Turning, he whispered, "All right, go on out. Turn right and go around the corner of the building. Don't make any noise. There still might be somebody watching the jail."

Johnson went first, tiptoeing along the walk with scarcely a sound except that of a squeaking board. Schwartz followed, with Jesse close behind, the shotgun cradled in his hands. If they made a break for it, he wouldn't hesitate. He'd open fire and at this range he couldn't miss, even in pitch darkness.

The weeds rustled as they made their way along the side

of the building. They reached the alley, still walking as if they were stalking some kind of game. Not until they had gone a full block did Jesse's taut nerves begin to relax slightly. Maybe they'd gotten away without being seen. Maybe they were going to make it after all.

Johnson and Schwartz shuffled along ten or fifteen feet ahead of him. Aware that they might try to get away when they reached the horses, Jesse said, "I held off once, but don't count on me holding off again. The minute one of you tries to get away, I'll cut you in two."

Neither man replied. They reached the edge of town. Here Jesse took the lead, checking often to be sure they were right behind, but not letting them get close enough to try rushing him.

He reached the horses. He took ropes from the saddles of two of them. He looped a rope around the neck of each of his prisoners, tied both ropes fast to his saddle horn, then coiled up the excess rope. He mounted, gathered up the reins of both the other horses, and rode out, taking a circuitous route around the town.

Reaching the other side of it, he headed north and east. Colorado City was still two days' ride away, but it looked as if he was going to make it now.

CHAPTER 14

Pawnee Bluffs lay at the eastern edge of the Rockies. To the east the high plains stretched away into infinity, sometimes rolling, sometimes flat, sometimes broken by gentle hills or occasionally by a rock-rimmed butte. To the west, foothills gave way to higher, rockier mountains that turned dark with timber at the higher elevations and on the north-facing slopes. Eventually the dark green of pine and spruce gave way to the lighter green of aspen and, at last, above timberline, the silken green carpet of tundra began. On the tops of the higher peaks was the never-melting snow, lying deep and crusted on the lee side of the mountain crests, where the winter winds had drifted it.

Jesse Marks angled gradually toward the Colorado City road, ten miles east of town. Travel would be easier on the road and when it got light he would be able to see farther and spot any pursuit more quickly.

He admitted the possibility that the sheriff's ruse had not fooled Reuben Lillard and the rest of the men from town. It was possible that they had only pretended to follow the sheriff, Hansen, and Espinosa. Wondering about that, he stopped his horse and listened. The two prisoners remained quiet, also listening.

Jesse heard nothing. He touched his horse's sides with his heels and moved ahead again. He let the horse pick his own way, guiding him only to the extent of keeping him headed north and slightly east.

For the first time, he began to think of what would happen
when he had lodged the prisoners safely in the Colorado
City jail. He'd go back to Pawnee Bluffs and would find himself just about as popular as a skunk. Sarah might even be
bitter toward him, and he guessed he couldn't blame her if
she was. Still, when a man took on a job and swore an oath,
he couldn't push it all lightly aside the first time a little pressure was put on him.

Climbing out of a gully, Johnson suddenly complained,
"Deputy, them ropes around our necks are too damn tight.
What if one of us was to fall off our horse?"

"You're not going to fall off your horse."

"It ain't easy holdin' on when the horse is lungin' up the
side of a gully. Not with our hands cuffed behind our backs."

"Fall off then and we'll save the hangman's fee."

"That's a hell of a way for a lawman to talk. Anyways,
how's it going to look if you come in with one of us dead from
a broken neck? Nobody will believe it was an accident, es-
pecially seeing you're so sweet on that girl we—"

Jesse said furiously, "Shut your goddamn mouth!"

The man's tone turned wheedling. "Sorry. No offense. It's
just that we got a damn long ways to go. My neck's already
raw from this rope chafin' it."

Jesse didn't reply. They rode in silence for another half
hour. Finally Johnson pleaded, "At least cuff our hands in
front so's we can hold the reins."

Jesse said, "Not a chance."

"Well, then cuff our hands in front so's we can hang on to
the saddle horn, an' keep from fallin' off. You hold the reins."

Jesse scowled in the darkness. He didn't want to do either
of these men the slightest favor. He said, "You're doing fine.
Grip the horse with your knees."

Johnson grumbled but didn't say anything more. Once, in

the next half hour, Jesse heard a short, whispered exchange between the two. He turned his head and said, "Shut up."

"How you going to make us shut up, deputy? How you going to do that now?"

Jesse kicked his horse's ribs. The animal broke into a trot and the ropes around the two prisoners' necks drew taut. As the reins tightened the prisoners' horses also trotted, matching the gait of Jesse's horse and loosening the ropes. Jesse said, "That's how. Next time I'll let go of your horses' reins. I'll yank you out of your saddles, both of you."

Johnson laughed softly. Once more he whispered something to Schwartz, something Jesse couldn't hear. He said, "Maybe you'd be doin' us a favor if you did. At least it would be over with."

Schwartz said anxiously, "Deputy, he's—"

Johnson broke in. "Deputy, you ain't going to marry that girl, are you? After what we done to her? She's—"

Something in Jesse's head went off like a bomb. He dropped the reins of both the prisoners' horses and spurred his own. The animal leaped ahead. The two ropes drew taut, and choked cries came from both prisoners.

They were yanked from their saddles and both hit the ground, sliding. Realizing what he had done, Jesse yanked his horse to a halt. As soon as he got enough slack in the ropes, he threw them off his saddle horn.

Both Johnson and Schwartz lay motionless on the ground. He had broken both their necks, thought Jesse, and he'd never be able to convince anybody that he, himself, hadn't deliberately hanged them both.

He left his horse, the ends of both ropes in his hands. Even as he did, he saw that neither of the prisoners was dead. Both were moving now, and moving swiftly. They had tricked him. They hadn't been yanked from their horses. They had leaped from them.

There was little light and Jesse could only see the shapes of the men against the lighter ground. Sitting, both men brought down their manacled hands. With legs doubled up, it was possible for them to bring their feet through, thus putting their handcuffed hands in front.

Instantly Jesse lunged back against the ropes, knowing that if he did not the first thing the prisoners would do would be to throw off the nooses. He had made a bad mistake. He had been deliberately goaded into doing what he'd done. It had been a desperate gamble by the prisoners, thus goading him, but they'd had absolutely nothing to lose. They knew they were going to die one way or another. No escape attempt was too desperate to be tried. No risk was too great to take.

He felt the ropes tighten. He pulled Schwartz, the lighter of the two prisoners, off balance. But Johnson had been quicker than Schwartz had. Johnson had managed to get his hands up, had managed to get them between his neck and the noose. Now he came lunging at Jesse, who could not continue to keep the noose tight because of Schwartz at the end of the other rope.

Seeing Johnson only half a dozen yards away and coming fast, Jesse dropped both ropes and grabbed frantically for his gun. His hand slapped the grips and he brought it out and up, cocking it as he did.

By now Johnson had succeeded in getting the noose loosened and over his head. Jesse raised the gun, finger tightening on the trigger.

Johnson veered aside. Jesse followed him with his gun. And then, completely unexpected, Schwartz's body hit him just above the knees, dumping him neatly to the ground.

Savagely he swung the gun. Its barrel connected with Schwartz's head. The man slumped and Jesse fought to his feet. But he was too late. Johnson was lost in the darkness. Jesse no longer had anything at which to shoot.

The horses! he thought frantically, and plunged in the direction he had last seen them. He blundered into one and seized the headstall even as the frightened animal plunged away. Being half dragged, Jesse saw the other one immediately ahead. Johnson was in the act of mounting him.

Jesse released the headstall. He raised his gun and fired, but he was falling even as he did, and knew that he had missed. By the time he got up, Johnson and the horse had vanished into the blackness of the night.

Jesse whirled and ran back to where Schwartz still lay. Jesse kicked him to see if he was conscious. Conscious, he would cry out. Unconscious, he would not. Schwartz made no sound.

Satisfied, Jesse ran to his own horse, put a foot in the stirrup, and hit the saddle as the horse began to run. He shoved his revolver back into its holster and withdrew the shotgun from the saddle boot.

Unsuccessfully probing the darkness ahead with his glance, he rode this way for several minutes, pushing his horse recklessly to his limit. Then he hauled back on the reins and brought the horse to a plunging, sliding halt.

The only sound now was that of the horse's breathing. Jesse listened intently. He heard nothing.

He stepped from his saddle, knelt, and put his ear to the ground. If Johnson's horse was still running, he would hear the sound. But, again, he heard nothing.

He mounted disgustedly, turned the horse and headed back toward the place where he had left Schwartz. Savagely and bitterly he cursed his own stupidity. He had fallen into their trap. He had let himself be baited and had done exactly what they had wanted him to do.

Schwartz was stirring. Jesse dismounted and tied both horses to scrubby clumps of brush. There wasn't one damn thing he could do. He couldn't trail Johnson in the dark. Pursuing him would have to wait until it was light enough to trail.

He said furiously, "Whose idea was that? Johnson's or yours?"

"His." Schwartz's voice was a whine. "I didn't want to go along with it but he said he'd kill me if I said anything."

"Liar!" Jesse irritably paced back and forth. He doubted if there was enough loyalty between the two men to make Johnson come back and try to rescue Schwartz, but he didn't dare assume it. He said, "Will he come back for you?"

Schwartz laughed bitterly. "Him! Hell, he don't give a damn for me. He's ten miles away from here by now."

"What'd you do to keep from getting your necks broke, jump from your horses?"

"Uh-huh. My neck's raw, though, now. Can't you take this damn rope off?"

Jesse said, "You go to hell. That rope stays right where it is."

"What you going to do, Deputy? Take me to Colorado City or go after him?"

Jesse said sourly, "Maybe I'll just string you up and then go after him. I'll have a better chance without you to slow me down."

Schwartz didn't reply, apparently believing this to be a time for silence. Jesse walked to Schwartz. He yanked him to his feet, unlocked the handcuffs, then led him to a scrubby tree and relocked the cuffs so that Schwartz's hands were around the tree. He took the rope off Schwartz's neck and coiled it up. He recovered the other rope and coiled it similarly.

Next he went to the horses, untied them, and picketed

them at the ends of the ropes. Rest and the chance to graze would make them both stronger tomorrow.

He returned to the place where he had left Schwartz. He sat down and put his back to a rock. It was going to take every bit of strength and skill he possessed to overtake Johnson and recapture him. And since there was nothing he could do until daylight, he'd just as well try to get some sleep.

He closed his eyes. He was keyed up and nervous. He saw Sarah in his mind, her bruised and battered face, her eyes red from weeping.

What if he didn't catch up with Johnson tomorrow? What if he lost the trail? As far as the people of Pawnee Bluffs were concerned, doing that would be ten times worse than simply taking the men to Colorado City for trial. Nobody in Pawnee Bluffs would ever forgive him if Johnson got away.

For an instant he seriously considered killing Schwartz. He could say later that he had killed the man during the escape attempt. And with Schwartz out of the way, his chance of catching Johnson would be vastly improved.

Yet even as he had the thought he knew it was something he couldn't do. He closed his eyes again and tried to calm his thoughts enough to sleep. But it didn't work and finally he gave up, contenting himself with simply resting with his back to the rock.

He found himself going over in his mind what had happened and ruefully realized he was preparing his defense against those who would criticize him for losing his prisoner.

He'd handcuffed their hands behind their backs, and that was right. He, himself, had held the reins of their horses, and that was right. To prevent exactly what had happened, he'd placed ropes around their necks and had secured the ropes to his own saddle horn. And that, also, was right.

The only wrong thing he'd done was to let their taunting get to him. And yet how could he have helped himself? Loving Sarah and planning to marry her, how could he have calmly taken the taunting Johnson had begun? And even if he had been able to take the initial taunting, it would have gotten worse.

What he should have done, of course, was stop and gag Johnson so that he couldn't talk. But he hadn't, and now it was too late. Anyway, there was no use rehashing things. What was done was done. Tomorrow he'd have to see if he couldn't catch Johnson and thereby put things right.

Schwartz, who had lain down on the ground, now began to snore. Jesse stood it for as long as he could. Then he got up, went to Schwartz, and savagely kicked him in the rump. Schwartz awoke with a start, complaining bitterly. Jesse asked, "How the hell can you sleep, you sonofabitch? After what you've done?"

Schwartz said, "I didn't throw them off that cliff. Johnson done that. All I done was—"

Jesse kicked him again. Schwartz didn't finish what he had been going to say.

Again, Jesse began to pace back and forth. He wished that he had a fire. He wished that he knew what time it was. Finally he shielded a match and by its light looked at his watch. It was a little after three.

Johnson would have at least a two- or three-hour start by the time daylight came, he thought. If the man really pushed his horse, that would amount to twenty miles.

Despair touched him. How was he going to make up twenty miles, encumbered as he was with Schwartz? The answer was that he wasn't. Unless something happened to close the gap. And there was more chance that something would happen to widen it.

Maybe both he and Sheriff Keogh had been wrong, he thought. Maybe they should have kept the prisoners in Pawnee Bluffs and if the townspeople insisted on lynching them maybe he and the sheriff should have permitted it. This way, considering what had happened, the town might get ripped apart even worse than a lynching could have ripped it apart. Furthermore, Johnson was loose, to rape and kill again.

Jesse involuntarily clenched his fists. Johnson wasn't going to kill again. Johnson wasn't going to get away. He would overtake the man no matter what he had to do. He'd handcuff Schwartz to a tree and leave him if he must. He'd kill the man if there was no other way.

He began to stare anxiously toward the horizon in the east. Half a dozen times he imagined that it was getting light, only to realize wishful thinking had made him think it was.

But at last the horizon in the east did show a faint line of gray. Sure of it this time, Jesse got up, went to the horses, and coiled the picket ropes. He saddled them and put on the bridles. He led them back to where Schwartz sat handcuffed to the scrubby tree.

He unlocked one cuff, then locked it again, this time with Schwartz's hands in front of him. He mounted his own horse and waited until Schwartz had mounted his. Then he rode close and put the noose around Schwartz's neck. He said, "Stay behind me, but by God keep up. This rope is going to be tied hard to the saddle horn. And if you try to throw it off, I'll shoot you down. Is that understood?"

Schwartz whined, "My neck is raw. Can't you . . ."

Jesse glared at him unfeelingly. He said harshly, "Every time it hurts you, just think about how you hurt that girl." He touched heels to his horse's sides and rode away in the direction Johnson had gone last night. Clear of camp, he stopped, waiting until it would be light enough to clearly see the ground.

CHAPTER 15

Sitting there on his fidgeting horse, Jesse scowled angrily to himself. As a practical matter he knew he ought to kill Schwartz now. With Schwartz slowing him, his chances of overtaking Johnson were slim. Without Schwartz, they were at least even and maybe a little bit better than that.

He would not be blamed, either by the people of Pawnee Bluffs or by Sheriff Keogh, if he killed Schwartz. He might even be praised.

The trouble was, he admitted sourly, that a man's own damn conscience wouldn't let him do certain things even though he knew others would approve. Killing Schwartz, however expedient, would be cold-blooded murder and Jesse Marks knew it would. That made it impossible.

But he wasn't going to let Schwartz slow him down. No matter how brutal he had to be, Schwartz was going to keep up. He wasn't going to lose Johnson, who had been the instigator of the attack on Sarah Lillard and who, according to Schwartz, had thrown both girls off the cliff.

Impatient and angry, he waited for the sky to grow light enough so that he could trail. Finally, too impatient to wait any longer, he got down and walked, at first bending low in order to see the ground. The rope that secured Schwartz was tied fast to the saddle horn. Frequently he glanced back to make sure Schwartz wasn't trying to get it off his neck.

Gradually the sky grew lighter and at last Jesse was able to mount his horse. The trail left by Johnson was, in daylight, plain and easily followed, and Jesse urged his horse to lope. Schwartz, able to control his horse now that his hands were cuffed in front of him, forced his animal to a speed that kept slack in the rope around his neck.

Johnson's trail, at first, led straight north across the rolling land. But, two or three miles from where he had escaped, he apparently had changed his mind about the direction in which he wished to go. The trail turned abruptly and headed west, up over the first of the rounded foothills and on to the steeper, rockier slopes beyond.

On rocky ground the trail became more difficult to follow and Jesse was forced to slow. Frustration began to grow in him. Johnson was apparently making no effort to follow watercourses where the going was easier. Up he went, and down, and up again, seeking out the roughest going where the ground was rocky or, later, where pine needles made a thick carpet on the ground that absorbed and all but hid his horse's tracks.

Once, the rope tightened on Schwartz's neck as Jesse's horse lunged up a particularly steep climb. The man cried out, and in desperation forced his own horse to a faster gait. Thereafter he made it a point to stay close behind Jesse and thus keep plenty of slack in the rope.

The horses sweated and their necks began to show white foam. Finally Jesse pulled them to a halt at the crest of a ridge, dismounted, and loosened the saddle girth. He curtly ordered Schwartz to do the same, cautioning, "You'd better keep your horse in shape. If he gets so he can't travel, I'm going to shoot both of you."

Schwartz loosened his cinch. He approached Jesse but stopped when Jesse said, "Keep your distance. Stay out near the end of that rope."

From here, Jesse could look eastward and see the vast plain stretching away into infinity. He wondered where the sheriff, Espinosa, and Hansen were, wondered if Lillard and his mob had overtaken them.

Something caught his eye. It was a long way off, ten miles at least. He squinted and kept his glance on it, finally deciding what it was. It was a lifting cloud of dust, made by many fast-moving men.

He studied it for a long time afterward, finally able to note movement, however slow it appeared from here. The dust cloud and those who made it were coming this way. They were still several miles from the first of the foothills, but apparently they had Jesse's trail and were following it.

Which meant they knew Johnson had escaped. Jesse thought how furiously angry Reuben Lillard must be. He wondered if the sheriff and his two deputies were with the group and decided it was unlikely that they were. What was more likely was that the three were traveling alone, trying to reach Jesse and his prisoner before Lillard could.

Not that Keogh wouldn't be just as furious with him for letting Johnson get away as Lillard was. Jesse looked critically at his horse. The animal was still heaving from the exertion. Jesse suddenly yanked off the saddle and began rubbing down the horse with the saddle blanket. Schwartz watched him for a moment and then reluctantly followed suit. Schwartz had apparently taken him seriously when he'd threatened to shoot both man and horse if they did not keep up.

Jesse finished rubbing down the horse, but he left off the saddle. He wanted desperately to get going, and was very conscious of the approach of Lillard and his mob of angry citizens. But he knew that too much haste now might result in losing Johnson altogether. If he wore out the horses, Johnson was going to get away. There weren't any ranches ahead that he knew of and it was unlikely that they'd encounter any loose horses until after they had crossed the Continental Divide.

Schwartz whined, "Can't I take this damn rope off my neck?"

"Leave it where it is."

"My neck's raw. By God, it ain't human to make a man wear something like this when his neck is raw."

Jesse reached for the rope, still secured to his saddle horn. "You want me to give it a yank?" Schwartz closed his mouth, his eyes scared. He started to put up his manacled hands to grab the rope, then changed his mind.

Jesse wondered if he would really have yanked the rope. He decided that he would. He felt no pity for Schwartz and all he had to do if he ever did start to pity him was to think of Melissa and Sarah, and that would be the end of it.

Finally the horses seemed to be sufficiently rested. Jesse said, "Mount up. I don't have to tell you to stay close."

Schwartz obeyed. His eyes, staring at Jesse, were ugly and filled with hate. He'd kill his captor without mercy if he ever got the chance, Jesse thought. So it was up to him to see that Schwartz never got the chance.

Down they went, the horses sliding, toward the bottom of this ridge. In the soft ground at the bottom, Johnson's trail was plain. Jesse dismounted to study it.

It was impossible to tell from the tracks whether the horse was being pushed too hard. But here, where the ground was soft, it was possible for Jesse to tell about how old the trail was. He had gained a little, he thought. The trail was, in his opinion, no more than three hours old.

He put his horse up the slope beyond. Occasionally he glanced back at Schwartz. Smiling grimly, he realized that he had put the fear of God in Schwartz. The man wasn't about to try what Johnson had tried. He was convinced that Jesse would shoot him down before he had gone fifty yards.

From each succeeding crest, Jesse studied the land ahead. Sooner or later Johnson was going to make a mistake. The higher these mountains got, the rougher they became. Sooner or later Johnson was going to ride into country so rough that he could not go on. He'd have to turn around and seek another way. When he did, Jesse would have a good chance of catching up with him.

He tried to remember the rivers that lay ahead. Aside from several small and unnamed streams, the first they were due to cross was Clear Creek, the one that ran through Pawnee Bluffs, and in which Melissa had drowned. Here in the mountains it ran deep and swift, chest deep on a horse. Its bottom was covered with rounded rocks, polished by the action of the water rushing over them. A horse trying to cross was almost certain to go down.

And if Johnson made it across this stream, another, worse one lay ahead. This one was Bear River, slower and bigger, fordable wherever it spread out, but treacherous where it did not.

Nor were rivers the only obstacles that might turn Johnson back. There were plenty of mountainsides ahead that a horse could not negotiate, being just too steep. There were timbered mountainsides where downed timber and the very density of the growth made it all but impassable.

Jesse tried to make himself relax. The terrain was in his favor. If he kept going as fast as he could consistent with saving the horses' strength, he would overtake Johnson eventually.

The morning dragged past slowly. Much of the time, now, they traveled in heavy timber. Johnson's trail zigzagged through it, circling dead trees lying on the ground, avoiding the thicker pockets where in places the trees grew less than a foot apart, making these thickets impenetrable.

As the altitude increased the air grew cooler, despite the sun beating down. At last, near noon, they reached the deep canyon of Clear Creek.

Jesse halted at the crest of the ridge and stared down into the gorge. Even from here he could hear the roar of the stream. He searched each square yard of the slope across from him, without success.

Wanting to be absolutely sure, he got down and studied the tracks of Johnson's horse. They appeared to be very fresh and he decided they could be from a few minutes to half an hour old. Johnson could be on the near slope still or he could have crossed already and climbed out over the far ridge.

Jesse touched his horse's sides with his heels and moved on down the side of the ridge. He hadn't spoken to Schwartz for a couple of hours, but had looked back at him frequently.

The roar of the stream grew louder as they got closer to it. Jesse suddenly became aware that the rope was dragging on the ground.

He snatched his revolver from its holster and whirled in the saddle. He tried to yank his horse to a halt but the animal couldn't stop because of the steepness of the descent.

Schwartz, counting on the roar of the stream to conceal the fact that he had stopped his horse, had thrown the rope off his neck. He was now kicking his horse frantically along a course parallel to the slope, rapidly drawing away from Jesse.

In another few moments he would be out of both pistol and shotgun range. Jesse didn't hesitate. He left his horse with one leap, withdrawing the shotgun from the saddle boot as he did. He struck the ground on both feet but immediately began to slide.

Frantically he grabbed a stunted tree and stopped himself. He raised his revolver and fired through the branches of a pine tree immediately above Schwartz's head. Pine needles and twigs dropped, some of them on Schwartz's head. Jesse roared, "You sonofabitch, the next one goes in your back!"

Schwartz dragged his horse to a halt. Jesse now had both feet braced. He holstered his revolver and brought the double-barreled shotgun to bear. At this range, with buckshot, he'd get both man and horse. But if Schwartz had gone another twenty-five or thirty feet . . .

Jesse yelled, "Turn him and come back!"

Schwartz turned his head. Jesse had never seen more virulent hatred in the eyes of another man. In a steady, even tone, Jesse said, "Make up your mind and make it up fast. I've got two barrels and you're going to get both of them. It don't make a damn bit of difference to me what you do, but do it in the next half minute or I'm going to let go!"

Schwartz hesitated for only a moment more. Then he dropped his glance from Jesse's and reined his horse around. He approached, and Jesse could see briefly in his eyes the thought that, if he spurred his horse suddenly enough, he might be able to run Jesse down.

Jesse said savagely, "Come on! Do it if you've got the guts!"

The thought went out of Schwartz's eyes. He reached Jesse, who said, "Get off the horse."

"What are you going to do?" Schwartz was fearful now.

"Let you walk, while I ride. Get down."

Schwartz dismounted reluctantly. Jesse said, "Back off."

Schwartz obeyed, backing off parallel to the slope in the direction in which he had ridden his horse a few moments before.

Jesse mounted Schwartz's horse. Sitting there with the shotgun trained on Schwartz, he ordered him on down the hill. His own horse stood at the bottom, beside the rushing stream, reins and rope trailing.

Schwartz headed down the hill, sliding, sometimes on his feet, sometimes on his rump. Jesse followed far enough behind so that he wouldn't overrun his prisoner.

He had lost Johnson and had no guarantee that he'd ever recapture him. He wasn't going to take another chance with Schwartz. The next time the man tried to escape, he was going to be dead.

CHAPTER 16

Sheriff Morgan Keogh, with Hansen and Espinosa following, rode at a walk, staying in the alley until they reached the lower end of town. Then Keogh crossed Pawnee, glancing upstreet as he did. He had to know if they had been seen and if they were being followed. Otherwise there was no point in leaving town at all.

The only light was in front of the Pawnee Hotel and Saloon. He saw two men leave to disappear into the darkness, and a few moments later saw three more. Softly he said, "They saw us. Let's go."

He led away, heading straight east, paralleling the course of the creek. He didn't hurry because he didn't want to lose whoever was following. Furthermore, he wanted to allow time for the pursuit to organize and catch up.

He hoped Jesse would wait until everybody had left town before trying to get the prisoners away. He had confidence in Jesse, but he knew he was putting an awesome responsibility on his deputy. Johnson and Schwartz were desperate and would try anything to escape. They knew that if they did not they surely were going to hang.

Nor was keeping custody of his prisoners Jesse's only problem. He was going to be alone with the two who had raped Sarah and thrown her off the cliff, with the ones who had murdered Melissa so that she couldn't tell. It would be an almost irresistible temptation to kill or otherwise mistreat the prisoners. Jesse would be no normal man otherwise.

Once, Keogh briefly heard galloping hoofbeats behind. The three horses plodded along and about five miles east of town, the three men struck a road. Afterward they followed it, but now speeded up the horses to a jogging trot. Keogh didn't want to be caught too soon. He wanted Jesse to have time to get away. But he figured he didn't have to worry about being overtaken too soon. Lillard would want to be at least a dozen miles from town before he overtook the sheriff and his prisoners. The farther from town the lynching took place, the less fuss there was going to be later because of it.

Shortly after striking the road, however, Keogh once again heard galloping hoofbeats behind. This time the sound continued, growing louder as the pursuers gained.

Keogh kicked his own horse into a lope. Espinosa and Hansen followed suit.

Hansen drew his horse abreast of Keogh's and yelled, "I feel like a sitting duck. What if they start shooting at us?"

Keogh yelled back, "They won't. They've got something worse in mind!"

"I wish I could be as sure of that as you are!"

"Don't worry. When they get close enough to hit us, we'll pull up."

Hansen dropped back. Keogh could hear him yelling something to Espinosa but, because of the speed at which they were traveling, didn't make out what it was.

He maintained a hard gallop until the horses were heavily sweated and faltering. Finally he pulled up. By now Jesse was a long way from town and nobody was likely to find his trail before daylight came. Even if they did, they wouldn't be able to follow it except at a dead-slow speed.

He told Espinosa and Hansen to get behind him in case any of the posse members were excited enough to shoot. When the galloping mob came in sight he bawled, "Hold it! Stop right where you are!"

They pulled their horses to a plunging halt. All except Lillard, Sauls, and Frank Fothergill. These three came riding forward and Lillard said harshly, "No use fighting us, Keogh. We're too many for you and we're going to have those two."

Keogh said, "Hansen and Espinosa? What do you want with them?"

There was a silence that seemed to last for a minute at least. When Lillard's voice came it was ugly and menacing. "What are you talking about?"

Keogh turned his head and said, "Speak up, you two. Tell Mr. Lillard who you are."

The response came immediately and from both men at once. To Lillard their voices were unmistakable and the knowledge that he had been made a fool of must have hit him like a thunderbolt because for once he didn't have anything to say.

The men behind him were also silent, stunned. Keogh shouted, "Go on back to town, boys. There's not going to be any hangings tonight."

A choked, gurgling sound came from Reuben Lillard's mouth. He was a man tormented. His older daughter had defied him and because of it she'd been raped and thrown off a cliff. His younger daughter was dead because she happened to have followed her sister out of sympathy. His wife had informed him that she was leaving him, taking Sarah with her, and Sarah had informed him that she was going to marry Jesse no matter what he said. To top it off, the man who more than twenty-five years ago had taken from him the only woman he had ever really loved had duped him and cheated him out of his vengeance against those who had killed one of his daughters and nearly killed the other one.

It was more than human flesh and blood could stand. Lillard savagely gouged his exhausted horse with his spurs and the animal leaped ahead. Reined hard to one side, he crashed into the sheriff's horse.

That movement was all Lillard required of the horse. He seized Keogh around the neck and as the two frightened horses drew apart, both men tumbled to the ground.

Keogh lit on his back, with Lillard on top of him and their combined weight coupled with the distance of the fall knocked every bit of wind out of him. Gasping, his chest afire, he still had enough presence of mind to bring a knee savagely upward into Lillard's groin.

Lillard brought his legs up protectively, and for an instant his hold on the sheriff loosened. Keogh broke free. He couldn't get up. All he could do was double up, try to protect himself, and hope he was able to draw breath into his lungs before Lillard damaged him too much.

Lillard rose, bent over from the pain spreading upward from his groin. He stumbled toward the sheriff and when he was close enough, kicked him mercilessly in the small of the back. The kick brought a grunt from the sheriff and a yell of protest from both Hansen and Espinosa. They might have interfered, but Galen Sauls and Jed Brown yelled simultaneously, "Stay out of it. Let 'em fight it out!"

Keogh finally got a breath of clean, pure air into his lungs. He rolled and scrambled away before Lillard could kick him a second time. He made it to his hands and knees. Lillard came rushing at him, trying to kick him again.

In Keogh there was suddenly the same savage exultation that must have been in Lillard when he'd begun the fight. Between these two rancor and hatred had smoldered for many years. Now it could all release itself.

Keogh, on hands and knees, came pushing upward and drove forward, his legs working like pistons. When he reached Lillard his head was belly high. It struck Lillard squarely and drove a monstrous gust of air from him. The impact, which was heard by every man gathered there, made both men rebound. Motionless, they stood for a moment a dozen feet apart.

But it couldn't long remain this way. Lillard rushed again, swinging a great, bony fist, and Keogh took it squarely in the middle of his face. His nose burst and sprayed blood. The blow stung and brought tears flooding to his eyes. Before, he had been glad that at last he had come to blows with Lillard. Now, stung, he began to fight with growing anger, trying to beat Lillard into the ground.

He swung his own hard fist and stunned Lillard with a blow on the ear that nearly broke his hand. Thoroughly angered, he continued to rain blows on the rancher and by his very intensity drove him back several steps before Lillard recovered enough to retaliate.

When Lillard did recover, they stood toe to toe, trading blow for terrible blow, each of which bruised, stunned, brought blood, and left its mark. Back in the crowd a man said in a hushed, awed voice, "Jesus, will you look at that!"

It must have frustrated Lillard terribly to see that he couldn't beat his hated adversary into the ground. Keogh was taking blow for blow and showing no sign of weakening. Abandoning the use of his fist, Lillard suddenly rushed Keogh, grasping him around the waist with his powerful arms and, by the momentum of his rush, bearing Keogh back. Keogh struggled, but he was off balance. The two fell at the side of the road and rolled into the ditch.

Lillard released Keogh now and grappled for his throat. His huge, powerful hands closed and in less than a second his thick thumbs had collapsed and closed the sheriff's windpipe, shutting off his air.

It came to Keogh with a shock. This was not just a fight that would end with both men bruised and battered but still alive. This was a fight to the death. Lillard meant to kill him and

Lillard's men would prevent any interference until it was too late.

Keogh grabbed Lillard's wrists and tried to yank them from his throat. He failed, not because he was less strong than Lillard was but because their positions served to magnify Lillard's strength while diminishing his own. Lillard was on top, bearing down with his weight and the strength of his arms, while Keogh was trying to pull away those hands, lifting up and pulling out.

Bright lights flashed before Keogh's eyes. His chest was afire and he knew that if he didn't free himself in the next few seconds he never would. He tried bringing up a knee, but Lillard avoided it.

Suddenly, with all the strength he could muster, Keogh arched his body, then whipped it, turning as he did. Lillard was rolled aside but he did not release his death grip on Keogh's throat. What he did do was lose the additional pressure his weight had made it possible for him to exert. And frantic desperation gave the sheriff's arms added strength. He yanked Lillard's hands from his throat and kneed Lillard in the belly. Lillard grunted with the pain of that and Keogh took advantage of the instant's reprieve to yank his gun and clip Lillard above the ear with it.

Lillard slumped and Keogh rolled away. He came to his hands and knees and stayed there for a moment, head hanging, gasping, trying to fill his lungs through his aching throat. He still had his gun in his hand and when he sensed men approaching he came to his feet, thumbing back the hammer. Sauls, Brown, and Fothergill stopped instantly. Keogh choked hoarsely, "Espinosa, bring me my horse."

Espinosa complied. Keogh holstered his gun and pulled himself into the saddle. He was covered with dirt and blood and he had never felt worse in his entire life. There were things he wanted to say but he didn't feel like saying them.

He turned his horse, rode around the silent group of men, and headed back toward town. Espinosa and Hansen silently followed him. Keogh kept swallowing, trying to ease the awful ache in his throat.

Sourly he thought that everyone back there would probably criticize him for using his gun to end the fight. He discovered that he didn't give a damn. The way he felt right now, he meant to see that the law came out on top no matter what he had to do. Besides, hitting Lillard with his gun had been no worse than Lillard's kicking him when he had been helpless on the ground.

The horses had rested somewhat while the fight was going on. Now, Keogh maintained a steady trot toward town, already thinking ahead. It was certain that Lillard and the others would pick up Jesse's trail and follow it as soon as daylight came. But knowing where Jesse was headed would give him an advantage over Lillard and the others. He ought to be able to find Jesse's trail before they did.

Espinosa and Hansen were silent for a long time, but finally Espinosa said, "That was some fight, Sheriff. What are you going to do now?"

"Get fresh horses. Get out of town so we'll be able to find Jesse's trail before they go."

"You want us to go along?"

"I sure do. I'm going to need all the help that I can get."

Reuben Lillard's first consciousness was of his aching, throbbing head. He opened his eyes. He could smell horses and dust and somebody was holding him in a sitting position.

He remembered the fight, suddenly, and asked hoarsely, "What'd he hit me with?"

"His gun barrel, boss."

"Is he gone?"

"Yeah. He rode back toward town."

Lillard struggled to stand, with Brown and Sauls helping him. He said, "Somebody get my horse," wincing with the pain each movement caused in his head.

Somebody brought his horse. He mounted as carefully as he could. He headed back toward town, holding his horse to a walk. Even so, his head throbbed terribly.

He had no consciousness of haste. There was plenty of time to return to town and get fresh horses before it got light enough to trail. Sauls asked, "Now what do we do?"

"Wait for morning. Pick up Jesse Marks's trail when it's light enough."

"Where do you think Jesse's headed, boss?"

"Colorado City. That's the only place for two hundred miles with a jail strong enough to hold them two."

"You think we can catch up with them?"

Lillard thought about that. Finally he said, "We'll all get fresh horses. Then I want you to take five or six men and head for Colorado City as fast as you can go. When you get to that ridge this side of it, spread out and wait. If they get away from us, maybe you can stop them there."

"Sure."

Lillard said, "The rest of us will wait just north of town. As soon as it's light, we'll cast around and find his trail."

After that nobody said anything. Lillard's head gradually began to improve. When they reached town he sent the men to get fresh horses for themselves. He sent Sauls to the livery stable to get fresh mounts for Brown, Sauls, and himself. He went into the saloon, which Ernst Halverson had opened as soon as they'd arrived in town.

Three drinks made his head feel much better, but he still felt terrible. When Sauls returned with the horses, he went out, taking the bottle and putting it into his saddlebag. He waited impatiently until all the men had gathered.

Time and weariness had taken the edge off their anger and

outrage. Lillard yelled, "Any of you that wants a bottle, go get it and tell Ernst to charge it to me!" They started to troop into the saloon but Lillard stopped them with, "I'll give five hundred dollars to the man that picks up the trail! I'll give another hundred to every man that's with me when we catch up with them!"

That brought a cheer from them. They hurried into the saloon and hurried out again. They eagerly mounted and followed Lillard out of town.

But he didn't lead them very far. He stopped a mile from town, dismounted, took a drink from the bottle in the saddle-bags, and then began to impatiently pace back and forth.

A hundred times in the next couple of hours he glanced toward the east. At last the sky began to gray. A line appeared where the horizon was.

By now most of the men were a little drunk. Between the liquor and the promise of a reward, their eagerness had returned. They were as anxious for it to get light as Lillard was.

As soon as it was light enough to see the ground, Lillard dispatched half of them toward the east, half toward the west, to look for the trail left by Jesse Marks and his prisoners. He told them to fire a gun when they discovered it. Then he sat down, put his throbbing head into his hands, and waited for the sound.

CHAPTER 17

With fresh horses under them, Keogh, Hansen, and Espinosa rode out of town immediately. Keogh knew that cutting Jesse's trail would be relatively easy since he already knew that Jesse had gone north with the prisoners. All they needed was enough light to see the ground.

Heading northeast, he rode two or three miles before he drew his horse to a halt. He and Jesse had ridden this way many times, shortcutting the road to Colorado City, which went straight east from Pawnee Bluffs before turning north. He guessed that Jesse would have followed the same route last night.

He felt awful. He dismounted, sat down, and put his back to a rock. He stared gloomily at Espinosa and Hansen. He was sick. He hurt and he wanted a drink. But he didn't even have a smoke, his pipe and tobacco having been lost in the fight.

Espinosa and Hansen tied all three horses, then sat down near to him. The predawn air was cold and Keogh began to shiver uncomfortably.

He tried to guess what Lillard and the men with him were going to do. They would know that Jesse had headed for Colorado City since that was the only place within reasonable distance where the jail was strong enough to hold the prisoners. They, also, would have to wait for daylight, but then they, too, would find Jesse's trail.

The thought of having to fight Lillard and most of the men

in town for the right to do his duty and enforce the law angered Keogh. It angered him that they weren't willing to trust him, and Jesse, to keep custody of the prisoners and see that they went to trial. In a courtroom. Properly and legally.

He closed his eyes and mumbled, "I'm going to sleep. One of you stay awake and let me know when it's light enough to trail."

His head reeled. But he had always had a faculty for sleeping whenever he had an opportunity and that faculty did not desert him now. He awakened with Espinosa shaking him, saying, "Sheriff, it is light enough."

Stiffly Keogh got to his feet. Every muscle hurt from the fight he'd had with Lillard last night. He staggered to his horse and swung to the animal's back. He said, "One of you go one way and one the other. When you find the trail, let out a yell."

He sat slouched in the saddle, waiting, wishing that he could go back to town and go to bed. He had waited no more than two or three minutes before he heard Espinosa's shout, "Sheriff! Here it is!"

He rode toward the sound of Espinosa's voice. Hansen caught up with him. The trail of Jesse's horse and those of his prisoners was plain. Keogh kicked his horse into a trot and followed it. At the first ridge, he stopped and turned in his saddle to stare back toward town.

He saw them coming, a couple of miles back, and kicked his horse into a fast trot again. But he had not gone more than a mile before he stopped a second time.

He stared down at the mass of scuffed and overlying tracks on the ground. He rode his horse forward slowly, motioning for the others to stay back. It wasn't hard to see what had happened here. He saw the marks where the two prisoners had hit the ground after being yanked from their saddles. They must have goaded Jesse until he could no longer control himself. Once they hit the ground, they had probably pretended to be unconscious or dead, because Jesse had dismounted and approached.

Then they had exploded into action. Keogh saw the bootheel marks where Jesse had lain back against the ropes. He saw the marks where he and one of the prisoners had gone down, struggling. And he saw the trail the other had made, escaping.

He cursed softly to himself. He studied the prints for a moment more to determine which prisoner had escaped. He decided it had been Johnson, whose feet were bigger. He beckoned to Espinosa and Hansen and said, "One of them got away from him. I figure he had to wait for daylight to follow, so they can't be too far ahead. Let's go."

At a trot, then, he followed the trail made by Johnson, escaping, and Jesse and Schwartz, following. It was desperately necessary, now, that he overtake Jesse before Lillard and his self-appointed "posse" did. Lillard would be so infuriated over Johnson's escape that he'd probably hang Jesse along with Schwartz.

Even he, Hansen, and Espinosa were in danger if Johnson had not been recaptured by the time Lillard and his men caught up.

Jesse Marks was as aware as the sheriff was of the situation's urgency. At the stream's edge he took the reins of Schwartz's horse and then forced both animals out into the current where Johnson had crossed earlier. He still had the rope around Schwartz's neck, so he had double insurance that the man would not get away.

Scrambling and fighting for footing, the two horses plunged toward the other side. Once, Jesse's horse slipped on the rocky bottom and fell, but he regained his footing almost instantly and all Jesse got was wet. Finally Jesse's horse lunged out on the bank and Schwartz's horse followed him.

The water shed by Johnson's horse as he had plunged up the bank earlier had not yet dried and Jesse knew they were getting close. He glanced back over his shoulder, looking vainly for pursuit, before he spurred his horse up the mountainside.

Schwartz clung to the saddle horn with his manacled hands. His eyes were scared now, as if he had some premonition of disaster. Jesse admitted that he had the same kind of premonition himself, but then nothing had gone right so far, and that probably would account for it.

On this slope there was timber and heavy brush and Jesse thought what an ideal place it would be for Johnson to ambush him. His progress and course would be marked by the crashing of brush. All Johnson had to do was wait, and jump Jesse when he was close enough so that he couldn't miss.

But Jesse didn't slow nor change course because he knew the danger behind him was at least equal to that ahead. He crested the ridge and stared back. He still could see no pursuit.

Here, on top of the ridge, he could see for a hundred miles. The spine of the continent stretched away in snow-capped peaks to right and left. Johnson's trail turned north here and went along the ridge, which dipped and climbed and dipped again. About three miles farther on it petered out.

The ground was relatively level here and Jesse forced the horses into a trot. His wet clothes and the wind on this high ridge made him shiver with the cold. His horse must also have been cold because he broke into a lope. Jesse did not try to slow him down.

Near the place where the ridge petered out, the land dropped precipitously, much the way it did west of Pawnee Bluffs where the two Lillard girls had been thrown off. Jesse could hear the roar lifting from the stream far below.

The pair swept along at a hard gallop less than a dozen feet from the precipice.

Jesse never knew exactly what happened because he wasn't looking back. Something must have made Schwartz's horse stumble. Perhaps he put a galloping hoof down upon a rock that turned with him. In any case, the reins in Jesse's hands were suddenly yanked out of them. He heard a high yell of surprise.

The first thing Jesse did was check the dally of the rope around his saddle horn. Satisfied that it was secure, he hipped around in the saddle and looked back.

He was in time to see, through a cloud of rising dust, the body of Schwartz catapulted over the precipice. Schwartz's horse was down, rolling. The horse followed Schwartz over and suddenly, where there had been man and horse an instant before, there was nothing but a rising cloud of dust.

Then, like a fiddle string, the rope snapped taut. Jesse's horse took an involuntary step in the direction of the pull, then steadied himself and stood, putting his weight against the strain.

Having already checked to see that the dally was secure, Jesse left the saddle instantly, knowing the horse would stand. He ran to the edge of the precipice and looked down.

It went straight down for more than three hundred feet. The horse was still in mid-air when Jesse reached the edge, turning over and over, legs spraddled out, kicking as if trying to regain balance that could never be regained. He struck the rocks at the bottom and for several moments it was as if he had struck silently. Then the smacking sound of the impact reached Jesse's ears.

All of this had taken less than a second, from the time Jesse had reached the edge. He turned his attention to Schwartz, hanging by his neck at the end of the rope. Somehow Schwartz had managed to get both his hands up and between the rope and his neck before he was catapulted off the edge. He now swung back and forth, striking the rock wall and scraping along it with each swing.

It fleetingly crossed Jesse's mind that Schwartz had caused his horse to stumble in some bizarre escape attempt, but even as he had the thought he knew it was impossible. Schwartz had had no control of his horse because Jesse had held the reins. This had not been an escape attempt, as he had so quickly suspected, but a bona fide accident.

Quickly he returned to his horse. He couldn't know whether Schwartz was still alive or not, but he knew it was possible that Schwartz's neck had not been broken because of the man's hands between his neck and the rope. He picked up his horse's reins and led him away from the precipice, speaking soothingly to the terrified animal. The rope slid tight over the sharp rocks. Jesse hoped it wouldn't break.

When he encountered resistance, Jesse stopped the horse, dropped the reins on the ground and left the horse facing toward the precipice, keeping strain on the rope and standing fast. He hurried to the edge.

By kneeling he could get his hands on Schwartz's shirt. He grabbed a double handful of the cloth and dragged the man up onto level ground. The first thing he did was loosen the noose and take it off.

Schwartz's head lolled limply from side to side as he did. The man's face was congested with blood, turning purplish. There was no rise and fall to his chest. Jesse picked up his wrist and felt for pulse but he knew it was useless even as he did. Schwartz had been hanged, just as surely as if there had been a scaffold here. He had dropped to the end of the rope and, despite his hands between the rope and his throat, the fall had snapped his neck, causing almost instant death.

Jesse squatted there, a little chill running along his spine. Involuntarily he glanced up at the sky. This was like punishment from heaven and, however Jesse scoffed at the notion, the chill in his spine did not go away.

With a shudder, he finally got to his feet. He dragged Schwartz's body a dozen feet from the cliff. He folded the man's hands on his chest and left him lying there, open eyes staring sightlessly at the sky. He coiled his rope and walked to his horse.

He wasn't sorry that Schwartz was dead. He was glad. Perhaps finding Schwartz's body would satisfy Lillard and shock the men from town into turning back. He didn't really think it would, but it was possible.

Staring back, he could see Keogh, Espinosa, and Hansen just coming over the ridge on the other side of the river gorge. He was tempted to wait for them but then changed his mind. It would take them an hour to get this far, an hour when Johnson would be getting farther away.

He mounted. He glanced once more at Schwartz's body, looking small and helpless in death. Maybe, if he had been more alert, he could have kept Schwartz from going off the edge. Maybe if he had not first checked the dally he would have been quick enough to yank Schwartz back.

Turning away, he decided it didn't matter much one way or the other. From the time he had participated in the crime against the Lillard girls, no other fate had been possible for Schwartz. If he had not been hanged here, dangling over a precipice, he would have been lynched by Lillard and the men from town. Or, if Jesse had managed to get him safely to Colorado City, he would have been convicted of the crime and hanged legally.

Maybe this was easiest of all on Schwartz. And now that the man was dead, Jesse discovered that he could think of him without anger or bitterness. He could even be glad, because now that Schwartz was off his hands he could concentrate on recapturing Johnson, the worst of the two.

He did not look back again. He kicked his horse into a fast trot and swept along the ridge to where it ended, about half a mile farther on.

Here, again, the trail went steeply down, to a timbered, grassy saddle, then climbed again. Beyond, by some twenty miles, the granite peaks rose to end in their snowy crests.

In the bottom of the next canyon there was a small stream with grassy banks. Johnson had stopped here to rest his horse. He had nervously paced back and forth, probably often staring backward along the trail he had made. Then he had ridden up the valley, which, like all drainages, headed westward toward the divide.

The trail was easily followed and the going was easier. Jesse alternately loped his horse, walked him, trotted him, walked, and loped again. He wanted to catch Johnson today if that was possible, because if he had the night to travel, Johnson could be on the other side of the divide by the time it got light tomorrow.

CHAPTER 18

Jesse Marks traveled in the narrow valley for a couple of miles before it began to widen. Johnson's trail was fresh now, the hoofprints of his horse deeply imbedded in the soft, moist ground. Maintaining his pace, Jesse finally rounded a steep shoulder of solid rock and could see, ahead of him, a small log cabin with a plume of smoke rising from the stone chimney at one end.

He stopped immediately and for a moment sat on his horse, staring at the place. Johnson's horse was tied in front, a saddle on his back. Jesse felt a surge of elation. He had run down his quarry. All that remained now was to capture him.

But he didn't move, studying the scene before him with suspicious, narrowed eyes. This was just too damned easy to be believable. Johnson knew he was being pursued, by Jesse, probably by the sheriff, and certainly by the father of the slain girl and a bunch of maddened townspeople howling for his blood.

Whatever else Johnson was, he wasn't stupid enough to let himself be caught this way. Along with his other animal attributes, he possessed enough animal cunning to make that impossible. What, then, was Jesse to believe?

Maybe, he thought, Johnson had set this up deliberately, counting on Jesse not to swallow it, counting on him to ride right in. Maybe he was waiting, even now, inside the cabin with a rifle in his hands. He wasn't armed when he'd escaped, but he almost certainly was armed now. There would have been at least a rifle or a shotgun in the cabin that belonged to its occupants.

He studied the place for a moment more. It was a lived-in cabin, not an abandoned one. That was obvious.

Finally Jesse shrugged. There was only one thing he could do. He had to try to reach the cabin. But he couldn't conceal and protect himself while he was doing it.

The meadow was almost bare, having been heavily grazed by the saddle horses belonging to the cabin's occupants. Even the scrubby bushes that lined the tiny stream had been mostly eaten off. Jesse dismounted and tied his horse to a small pine tree. He slid his rifle from the scabbard, satisfied himself that his revolver was seated firmly in its holster, then suddenly sprinted for the stream.

He expected gunfire immediately but it didn't come. He flung himself flat beside the stream, partially sheltered by its shallow bank. Why hadn't Johnson fired, he wondered. The range had not been too great.

He began to crawl, slowly and laboriously, upstream, trying to stay low enough to avail himself of the protection offered by the shallow bank. Sometimes he had to go into the icy stream to keep himself concealed. Wet and cold and muddy, he finally reached a spot fifty yards from the front door and raised his head.

Everything was exactly as it had been before. The horse stood drowsily at the hitchrail. A thin plume of smoke rose from the chimney. Otherwise, nothing moved. The corral out back was empty, its gate ajar.

Jesse raised his head a little higher, feeling a chill running along his spine. What was Johnson waiting for? Why hadn't he fired? The range was only fifty yards, and at that range a man's head would be easy enough to hit.

The cabin door was slightly ajar and suddenly it moved. Jesse ducked down instantly, expecting the crack of a rifle.

No sound came. He risked a peek, and saw the door swing back. The smoke from the chimney was blowing away horizontally on a breeze that had suddenly come up.

He raised his head again, beginning to suspect that Johnson had already gone. Maybe he had taken a horse belonging to whoever lived here, and maybe he had taken a saddle, too, leaving his own standing out front to make Jesse do exactly what he just had done—waste half an hour sneaking up on the cabin for fear of getting shot.

Jesse suddenly leaped to his feet. Bending low, rifle carried in both hands in front of him, he ran, weaving from side to side, toward the cabin door.

He hit it with his shoulder, slammed it back, and burst inside. He tripped over something yielding and sprawled headlong on the packed earth floor, striking his head on the table leg. Rolling, he brought his rifle muzzle swinging around, prepared to shoot if Johnson was really here.

But nothing moved. No one stood by the cabin's front windows. Jesse got slowly to his feet. The body of an old man lay on the floor between him and the door. The man had been bludgeoned with something and he was dead.

Jesse let his glance circle the cabin. There was a bunk against the rear wall. An elderly woman lay on the bunk. She had been shot in the chest and was dead, too. Johnson was gone.

By now Jesse was chilled thoroughly. He went to the stove. It wasn't hot but it was warm. He bent over it, soaking up its heat, shivering. Johnson had fooled him with the horse tied out front. He'd done exactly what Johnson had wanted him to do.

Even as cold as he was, he didn't dare waste any more time here. The sheriff was coming and he'd see that these two got buried properly. Jesse had to go on and catch Johnson before he got across the divide.

He grabbed a blanket off the foot of the bunk. He wrapped it around his shoulders, Indian style, and hurried out the door. He untied and mounted Johnson's horse, then rode to where he had tied his own. He changed horses. Leading Johnson's horse in case something happened to his own, he rode out again.

Johnson's trail went on up the valley, which continued to widen. Jesse passed a small haystack that had a barbed wire fence around it to keep the livestock out.

Why the hell, he wondered, had Johnson felt it necessary to kill the helpless old couple who had owned this place? They could have been no threat to him.

Perhaps the old man had pointed his gun at Johnson. Perhaps the only way Johnson had been able to get it had been to hit the old man when he wasn't expecting it. But killing the man's wife had been an act of pure viciousness, like throwing the Lillard girls, alive, off the cliff.

As he rode Jesse wondered how many others had died because of Johnson's viciousness. How many did a man like that kill in his lifetime before somebody managed to kill him? Thirty? Forty? Maybe even more. Johnson had killed three in the last couple of days.

Several miles beyond the cabin, the valley began to narrow and climb. It ended in a shallow box canyon, its stream borne here as a trickle from an underground spring.

Johnson's trail climbed out, still heading west. Jesse's horse began to sweat so he changed mounts and rode Johnson's horse for a while. He hit the valley of Bear River in late afternoon, growing more nervously conscious of the swiftly passing time. He descended into the Bear River Canyon and rode his horse across where Johnson had, at a shallows where the river spread, ran smooth, and was less than three feet deep. He climbed the far slope and at the crest was able to see the lifting, bare slopes of the high peaks ahead.

The trail followed the ridge west of Bear River, struck another steep drainage and afterward followed that through timber growing ever more stunted and twisted the higher the drainage went.

The sun was low in the western sky when Jesse finally spotted his quarry ahead of him. Johnson was well above timberline, toiling upward across an all but denuded slope toward the snowy peak beyond.

Jesse changed horses swiftly and spurred his own horse into a lunging gallop. The summit lay less than three miles beyond where Johnson was, and Jesse was three quarters of a mile behind. He was nearly out of time.

He kept to the concealment of whatever rocks, timber, and natural draws were available, hoping Johnson wouldn't see him yet. Finally, half an hour after sighting Johnson, he broke out of the last clump of timber and was exposed.

Both of his horses were sweating heavily and breathing hard. Despite the blanket, Jesse was chilled all the way to his bones. He just had to catch Johnson tonight, before he crossed the divide and dropped down on the other side. If he didn't, the man was going to get away.

Savagely he spurred his horse onward across the high tundra toward the snowy peaks. He had succeeded in closing the distance between them to a quarter mile. Johnson was heading toward a kind of saddle between two peaks. Jesse angled toward it and spurred his horse. He drew his rifle and snapped a shot at Johnson, not with any expectation of hitting him but to make him turn aside.

The report rolled forward and back and to both sides, and returned as echoes from nearby slopes and peaks. Johnson turned his head. He saw Jesse and did exactly what Jesse wanted him to do. He veered aside, knowing that if he did not Jesse would close the distance between them to the range of a rifle before he could reach the saddle toward which he was riding.

Jesse now had him headed straight upward, toward the peak. He didn't know how much good it was going to do, if any, but he was familiar with these mountains if not with this particular peak. He knew that oftentimes a peak will be gently sloped on one side, and drop precipitously on the other.

Jesse's horse was tiring, faltering. Quickly he left the saddle and mounted Johnson's horse, which he had ridden very little during the afternoon. He left his own horse behind and spurred Johnson's horse angrily.

Desperately he hoped he had been right in guessing that the other side of this peak would be a precipitous descent. He'd know in a minute. Johnson had almost reached its crest.

Slightly less than a quarter mile behind his quarry, Jesse saw him reach the crest and halt. Johnson turned his head and stared back toward his pursuer. Then he turned his horse and galloped toward his right, savagely raking his horse's sides.

A small smile of satisfaction touched Jesse's mouth. He had guessed right. He instantly changed course to one that would intercept Johnson long before he could reach the saddle toward which he had originally been headed.

The distance between them began to close rapidly. Jesse raised his rifle, sighted as carefully as he could, and snapped another shot at the fleeing man. His aim was better than he had any right to expect. Apparently he creased Johnson's horse in the chest because suddenly the animal reared.

Johnson gave up trying to get away. He left his horse's back, carrying a rifle. He sprinted for a cluster of rocks nearby. He dived behind them before Jesse could fire again.

Jesse left his own horse as quickly as Johnson had left his, acutely aware that there was no cover for him here and that he was well within the range of Johnson's rifle. He threw himself down, flattening himself in the scrubby growth that covered the ground to a height of six inches but no more. Johnson's rifle cracked. The bullet dug into the ground several feet ahead of Jesse, showering him with dirt.

Desperately he glanced right and left. There was a slight depression a dozen feet to his right. He had to reach it, and quickly, or be killed.

He didn't dare rise and sprint for it. So instead he rolled, fast, toward it. Johnson's rifle cracked again, and again, its report echoing back from the nearby peaks, its bullets striking inches behind Jesse as he rolled.

Six feet. Four. Johnson's rifle cracked again and Jesse felt the burn of the bullet along the muscles of his back. Then he rolled into the depression where Johnson's bullets could not find him and lay there, bathed with sweat despite his still-damp clothes, despite the cold wind sweeping out of the west across this high and barren place. He was trembling violently and out of breath, content for these few moments to rest, regain his breath, and try to decide on his best next move.

Almost at once he knew what it was. The advantage was his in that Keogh, Espinosa, Hansen, Lillard, and the men from town were coming and would be arriving before it got completely dark. All he really needed to do was hold Johnson here.

Cautiously he raised his head. Johnson's horse stood, head hanging, less than fifty feet from the rocks where Johnson had holed up. Jesse slid his rifle out in front of him. He jacked in a cartridge and took careful aim on the neck of Johnson's horse.

He squeezed off the shot carefully. The horse went to his knees instantly as the bullet struck. He crumpled then, and when he hit the ground rolled over on his side.

Immediately Johnson began yelling, cursing, calling Jesse every foul name he knew. Jesse shifted his rifle, taking aim on the rocks where Johnson was, hoping the fugitive would show himself. The echoes of the shot were still coming back when Johnson's rifle barked.

No bullet struck near Jesse and for a moment he couldn't figure what Johnson had been shooting at. Then, suddenly, he knew. He could hear the horse which Johnson had left behind at the cabin and which he had brought here, thrashing around nearby on the ground. Enraged at the killing of his own mount, Johnson had taken revenge by killing the horse Jesse had ridden here. Now both of them were afoot, unless one or the other could reach the worn-out horse Jesse had abandoned a quarter mile behind.

Lying there with time to think, at last, Jesse knew that he had failed the task the sheriff had given him. Keogh had sent him to deliver the prisoners to Colorado City for trial. Now one was dead, the other pinned down on this high peak, and Lillard and the maddened mob from town would be arriving soon. He and Keogh were no better off than they had been back in town.

As far as he was concerned the only thing he had done here was make sure that Johnson would not escape again, but he discovered that that accomplishment gave him little to congratulate himself about. All he could think was that two innocent people were dead because he had let Johnson get away from him earlier.

CHAPTER 19

With a shock Jesse realized that the sun had already set. There were a few clouds in the sky, and the sun now stained them brilliant orange. He wondered how long it would be before Keogh arrived. And how long after that before Lillard and his mob of angry men arrived.

He tried to remember how many minutes it was between the time the sun went down and the time it became too dark to see. He'd never paid any attention to that particular span of time before, but now it made a difference.

Of one thing he was sure. As soon as it was dark enough, Johnson was going to make an attempt to escape. And just before that time came, he was going to rush the fugitive and either recapture him or kill him before he could get away.

Looking back, he saw Keogh come galloping up the slope. Keogh was alone and Jesse supposed he had left Hansen and Espinosa behind at the cabin to bury its murdered occupants. As he passed Jesse's horse, Keogh bent over and scooped up the reins. He came on, trailing Jesse's horse.

He pulled both horses to a halt far enough back to be out of Johnson's rifle range, having seen the two dead horses not far from where Jesse had holed up. He cupped his hands around his mouth and roared, "Jesse?"

Without raising his head, Jesse shouted back, "Yeah! I'm here!" He raised his gun and waved it without showing himself.

"Where's Johnson?"

"Holed up behind those rocks near the summit! He can't go on because it's a cliff!"

There was a moment's silence. Then Keogh roared, "Johnson?"

Johnson didn't bother to answer, but Jesse knew that he had heard. Apparently the sheriff thought so, too, because he bawled, "Give yourself up! Schwartz is dead and that mob is only half a mile behind!"

Johnson didn't answer him. Jesse couldn't really blame him because in Johnson's mind Keogh and Jesse had no better chance of protecting him from the mob now than they'd had before.

Johnson knew that this was the end of the line for him, that this was where he was going to die, and Jesse couldn't blame him for wanting to die by gunfire rather than by hanging or being dragged at the end of a rope.

The clouds had begun to fade from orange to gold. Jesse supposed that in less than ten minutes they would turn gray. Darkness would follow five or ten minutes after that.

Jesse didn't like his own and Keogh's position worth a damn. The way things stood, there was no way the law could win. There seemed to be only two ways this could turn out, and both were unacceptable. Johnson would either get away or be lynched.

From behind Keogh, now, he faintly heard the sound of shouting voices and the pound of horses' hoofs. Putting his ear to the ground made the hoofbeats seem like a dull thunder in the ground. Pink and violet touched the clouds, and Jesse knew that soon the sky would all be gray.

Raising his rifle, he motioned toward his right with it, hoping that Keogh would understand. After several moments he risked raising his head to look. Keogh was moving to Jesse's right, leading both horses.

The sound of approaching men was louder now, and more

of the dwindling light had faded from the clouds. Aware that time was nearly gone, Jesse leaped to his feet and sprinted to his left. Immediately Johnson's rifle opened up, but all of the bullets missed because of the fading light.

The gunshots brought shouting from the approaching mob. Jesse flung himself down in a slight depression, then raised his head enough to see. The mob broke from the scrubby timber where timberline began, riding at a gallop, spreading out into a long and straggly line.

Keogh, having dropped the horses' reins back out of Johnson's rifle range, had managed to get closer to Johnson's place of concealment while Johnson had been shooting at his deputy.

Jesse thought, with small satisfaction, that at least he and Keogh were now in position to prevent Johnson's escape. Not that it mattered. When the mob got here the whole thing would be taken out of their hands. Lillard would take over and the mob would have its way and everything he and Keogh had done to try to get Johnson tried legally would be wasted.

The thought of that made him mad. He was tired, and cold, and hungry, and it was going to be a long time before he was warm and rested and before he got fed again. He had been breaking his back to do what the people of Pawnee Bluffs paid him to do ever since the crime had been discovered. Simply doing his job had brought him here.

Schwartz's death had been an unavoidable accident and he was foolish to blame himself for it. But, by God, Johnson wasn't going to get away and Johnson wasn't going to be lynched. Pawnee County had chosen Keogh as its sheriff and Keogh had chosen him to be his deputy. Jesse intended to do his job even if some of the citizens of Pawnee County got hurt.

But how? For God's sake, how? Even now the mob followed Lillard up the slope, a solid wall of angry men, waving guns, shouting, cursing, acting like dogs that have finally cornered their helpless prey.

Johnson began shooting as soon as they were in range. A horse went down, throwing his rider clear. The man sprinted for a hollow and threw himself to the ground. Another man, hit, gave a high yell and pulled his mount to a halt. He wheeled his horse and rode back out of Johnson's range.

Johnson kept firing. Two more horses went down, despite the poor shooting light. And, as suddenly as it had formed, the charge faltered and turned aside. Men threw themselves behind the downed horses and opened fire on Johnson's pile of rocks. Those who could found cover in small depressions similar to the one in which Jesse lay. The others galloped out of range.

The sky was now wholly gray. Jesse risked raising his head and looked toward Keogh. The sheriff had his head up, looking toward his deputy.

Both of them seemed helpless, but somehow Jesse didn't like admitting their helplessness. There ought to be something. Maybe nothing was going to work, but he wasn't going to give up without a try.

Suddenly, without thinking about it anymore, he got to his feet. He made a good target, and Johnson lost no time opening fire on him. As he charged recklessly toward the pile of rocks behind which Johnson had concealed himself, Jesse had the wry thought that he must be crazy to be doing a thing like this. He would get himself killed, and for nothing because in the end Johnson was going to be lynched anyway.

No. Not for nothing. Jesse hadn't been looking for just any job when he'd signed on as Keogh's deputy. He'd been looking for something more. Believing that people have a right to be secure, to be safe from those who would prey on them, he knew that only the law and the men enforcing it were able to guarantee that right.

Now he was pitting himself against the people he had taken an oath to protect. But the law was, or should be, impartial, if nothing else. When it was broken it didn't matter who had broken it.

He was running, zigzagging frantically from side to side, and he could, in the gathering darkness, see the flashes of Johnson's rifle ahead. He heard Keogh bawl, "You damn fool! What the hell do you think you're doing, anyway?"

The men who comprised the mob were suddenly as silent as Keogh was vocal. Keogh bawled, "Come back!" but when he saw his commands were having no effect, he set himself a practical chore—that of keeping Johnson's head pulled down. He began firing his rifle as fast as he could work the lever. Jesse heard several bullets strike the rocks where Johnson was and afterward whine away into space.

He was more than halfway there when Keogh stopped firing. Jesse hadn't counted Keogh's shots, but he knew the gun had to be empty or Keogh would not have stopped.

He now was less than fifteen feet from Johnson. The man rose, took aim, and fired before Jesse could veer aside.

Something like a mule's kick struck Jesse's thigh. Johnson's gun flashed again, missing this time because Jesse was already on his way down. The leg folded under him and the next instant he was flat on the ground.

Blood, warm and wet, soaked his thigh almost instantly. He thought with surprise, "I'm hit!" but because this was a hell of a place to be wounded and motionless, he began crawling, dragging the numb and almost useless leg behind.

Johnson's gun, too, must have run out of cartridges, because for a few seconds it was silent. Keogh was still yelling at Jesse, but Jesse's mind didn't seem able to sort out the words and make sense of them. All he could think was that, by God, he was going to reach Johnson and take him prisoner.

Less than ten feet from Johnson's rocks, Jesse suddenly

put his rifle down to use as a prop and forced himself to his knees and then to his feet. The wounded leg was nearly numb, but he could feel the warm wetness of the blood and knew that feeling was a hopeful sign. He put his weight on it gingerly and discovered that if he was careful, it would support his weight.

Apparently Johnson now had his gun loaded, because he raised it in the near-darkness and took aim. Jesse's time was gone. In an instant, the gun would flash and at this range Johnson couldn't miss.

He dived at Johnson's legs. The gun fired, but the bullet went harmlessly into thin air where Jesse had been less than a second before. Jesse's body struck Johnson's legs even as the man gave up trying to fire it and swung it like a club.

It came down across Jesse's back with enough force to drive him to the ground again. But the force of his body striking Johnson's legs sent the man staggering back, trying desperately to stay erect.

Jesse raised his head and forced himself to his hands and knees. There was a steep slope several yards behind the rocks, and then the void, black as a pit. Jesse didn't know whether Johnson realized he was going over. The man fell, and his arms went out, his fingers digging, like claws, into the rocky ground. Jesse made an involuntary movement toward the man to try to grab him, but he was too late. Johnson was sliding now, sliding toward the rim, and Jesse could do nothing but watch.

And then suddenly Johnson simply wasn't there. A high yell, almost like a scream, lifted from the void, diminished, and then was gone. All that was left was the bitter wind sweeping across the peak, and the grating sounds of Keogh's feet as the sheriff ran toward him.

Jesse's head whirled. He made it to his feet and walked toward the sounds of the sheriff's feet, using his rifle as a cane.

It was over. They had failed in their efforts to bring Johnson and Schwartz to trial, but they had succeeded in preventing them from being lynched. And he couldn't help thinking how just it was that these two men, who had callously thrown two helpless girls off a cliff, should die by the same means.

Lillard was issuing orders for men to go to the foot of the peak after Johnson's body. Keogh put his arm around Jesse and held him up. He said, "That was a damn fool thing to do."

Jesse didn't answer. He was dizzy and thought he was going to pass out. Keogh said, "But I'm glad you did it. You done them out of their lynching, anyway."

Jesse collapsed. When he came to they were back in the timber and a fire was burning close to him. He was warm and drowsy but he was hungry, too. Keogh saw that he was awake and said, "Flesh wound. You'll make it. Think that you can ride?"

Jesse nodded drowsily. Keogh said, "Lillard and the others went back to town. I figured you and me would wait until it got light."

Jesse stared at the coffee and Keogh poured a cup. He put it on the ground, then raised Jesse and propped him against a tree. He picked up the cup and handed it to him.

Jesse knew nothing more would ever be said about what had happened here tonight. But he had the satisfying feeling that he had done his job as well as it could have been done. He had the feeling that Keogh thought so, too.

He wanted to see Sarah and he wanted to get back to town. Sipping the coffee, he waited impatiently for dawn.